Jessica Thought the Girl Looked Familiar . . .

Sitting on the sofa, Jessica turned her attention back to the movie. Three young kids were riding their bikes up a hill when they came upon a strange, eerie light behind a tree.

Jessica took a sip of her juice and watched as the three children jumped off their bikes and headed toward the strange light. As they stepped nearer, there was a closeup of their frightened faces.

Suddenly Jessica leapt out of her chair, spilling juice down the front of her robe. "That's her!" she cried. "I can't believe it!"

Jessica knelt in front of the television screen, waiting for another closeup of the children. Finally she nodded excitedly. "That's Maria!" She pointed to the girl on the screen. "Maria Slater! I just met this girl yesterday!"

Jessica sat back on the carpet, recalling her brief conversation with Maria. What was she doing in Sweet Valley? And why hadn't she revealed her true identity?

Bantam Skylark Books in the SWEET VALLEY TWINS series
Ask your bookseller for the books you have missed

#1 BEST FRIENDS
#2 TEACHER'S PET
#3 THE HAUNTED HOUSE
#4 CHOOSING SIDES
#5 SNEAKING OUT
#6 THE NEW GIRL
#7 THREE'S A CROWD
#8 FIRST PLACE
#9 AGAINST THE RULES
#10 ONE OF THE GANG
#11 BURIED TREASURE
#12 KEEPING SECRETS
#13 STRETCHING THE TRUTH
#14 TUG OF WAR
#15 THE OLDER BOY
#16 SECOND BEST
#17 BOYS AGAINST GIRLS
#18 CENTER OF ATTENTION
#19 THE BULLY
#20 PLAYING HOOKY
#21 LEFT BEHIND
#22 OUT OF PLACE
#23 CLAIM TO FAME
#24 JUMPING TO CONCLUSIONS
#25 STANDING OUT
#26 TAKING CHARGE
#27 TEAMWORK
#28 APRIL FOOL!

#29 JESSICA AND THE BRAT ATTACK
#30 PRINCESS ELIZABETH
#31 JESSICA'S BAD IDEA
#32 JESSICA ON STAGE
#33 ELIZABETH'S NEW HERO
#34 JESSICA, THE ROCK STAR
#35 AMY'S PEN PAL
#36 MARY IS MISSING
#37 THE WAR BETWEEN THE TWINS
#38 LOIS STRIKES BACK
#39 JESSICA AND THE MONEY MIX-UP
#40 DANNY MEANS TROUBLE
#41 THE TWINS GET CAUGHT
#42 JESSICA'S SECRET
#43 ELIZABETH'S FIRST KISS
#44 AMY MOVES IN
#45 LUCY TAKES THE REINS
#46 MADEMOISELLE JESSICA
#47 JESSICA'S NEW LOOK
#48 MANDY MILLER FIGHTS BACK
#49 THE TWINS' LITTLE SISTER
#50 JESSICA AND THE SECRET STAR

Sweet Valley Twins Super Editions
#1 THE CLASS TRIP
#2 HOLIDAY MISCHIEF
#3 THE BIG CAMP SECRET

Sweet Valley Twins Super Chiller Editions
#1 THE CHRISTMAS GHOST
#2 THE GHOST IN THE GRAVEYARD
#3 THE CARNIVAL GHOST

SWEET VALLEY TWINS

Jessica and the Secret Star

Written by
Jamie Suzanne

Created by
FRANCINE PASCAL

A BANTAM SKYLARK BOOK
NEW YORK · TORONTO · LONDON · SYDNEY · AUCKLAND

RL4, 008–012

JESSICA AND THE SECRET STAR
A Bantam Skylark Book / July 1991

Sweet Valley High® and Sweet Valley Twins are trademarks of
Francine Pascal

Conceived by Francine Pascal

Produced by Daniel Weiss Associates, Inc.
33 West 17th Street
New York, NY 10011

Cover art by James Mathewuse

Skylark Books is a registered trademark of Bantam Books, a division of
Bantam Doubleday Dell Publishing Group, Inc.
Registered in U.S. Patent and Trademark Office and elsewhere.

ISBN 0-553-15911-9

Published simultaneously in the United States and Canada

Bantam Books are published by Bantam Books, a division of Bantam
Doubleday Dell Publishing Group, Inc. Its trademark, consisting of
the words "Bantam Books" and the portrayal of a rooster, is Regis-
tered in U.S. Patent and Trademark Office and in other countries.
Marca Registrada. Bantam Books, 666 Fifth Avenue, New York,
New York 10103.

PRINTED IN THE UNITED STATES OF AMERICA

OPM   0 9 8 7 6 5 4 3 2 1

Jessica
and the
Secret Star

One

◇

"I just don't get it!" Jessica Wakefield shouted, slamming her English book shut.

"Get what?" Elizabeth, her twin sister, asked.

"This poetry stuff," Jessica moaned.

"Mr. Bowman assigned those poems on Friday," Elizabeth reminded her sister. "Maybe you'd understand them better if you hadn't waited to read them until homeroom Monday morning."

Jessica sighed and reopened her book. "They're full of *thees* and *thous*," she complained. "Why couldn't the authors just say *you*, like normal people?" Jessica looked at her twin for sympathy, but it was no use. Elizabeth actually enjoyed poetry; in fact, English was her favorite subject.

At times like this, it was hard for Jessica to

believe that she and Elizabeth were identical twins. True, they looked exactly alike. Both girls had sparkling blue-green eyes, long, sun-streaked blond hair, and a dimple in their left cheeks. But one thing made the twins easier to tell apart these days. Jessica was the twin who wore glasses occasionally.

Another difference between the twins was their personalities. Elizabeth loved to read, and her dream was to become a professional writer. She devoted much of her free time to working on the *Sweet Valley Sixers*, the sixth-grade newspaper that she had helped found. But mostly Elizabeth loved curling up with a good book, or talking with a close friend.

Jessica loved talking to her friends, too. She spent hours on the telephone each night, listening to the latest gossip from her friends in the Unicorn Club. The Unicorns were an exclusive group of the most popular girls at Sweet Valley Middle School. In fact, the Unicorns tried to wear something purple every day, to remind everyone of their special status.

"Did you hear the latest?"

Jessica looked up from her English book to see Caroline Pearce sitting down at the desk next to her. Caroline was the school's biggest gossip, but her information usually wasn't accurate.

"Probably," Jessica replied, tossing her hair over her shoulder.

"There's a new girl in school," Caroline whispered loudly enough for everyone to hear. "A sixth grader. And she's going to be in our homeroom."

"Sure, Caroline," Lila Fowler said with a smirk as she settled into the desk behind Jessica. "Look, Jessica. My dad went to New York last week and brought me back these bracelets." Lila jangled three thin purple bracelets near Jessica's ear. Next to Elizabeth, Lila was Jessica's best friend. She was the daughter of one of the wealthiest men in Sweet Valley, and she enjoyed reminding everyone of that whenever she could.

"I don't have to look," Jessica said, annoyed. "I can hear them."

"Don't you want to hear about the new girl?" Caroline pressed eagerly. "Her name is Maria—at least I think that's her name."

"Oh, yeah. Elizabeth, Amy, and Mandy saw her when she visited school last week. They said she's really pretty and wears funky clothes," Jessica said, pleased to know the scoop.

The bell rang just as Mr. Davis walked in. "Morning, folks. Before I take roll," he said, "I wanted to let you know that a new student will be joining us today. Her name is Maria Slater and—" Mr. Davis paused. "Why, there she is now!" He glanced at a girl who stood hesitantly in the doorway. "Come in, Maria. You may take the empty seat in the first row."

Jessica studied Maria with interest. She was a tall, strikingly pretty black girl, with wide brown eyes and a shy smile. She was wearing large gold earrings and a suede skirt—just like the one Jessica had admired in the latest issue of *Teenager*. And there was something strangely familiar about her. Jessica had the feeling that she had met Maria before.

"So, where are you from, Maria?" Mr. Davis asked.

Maria smiled shyly. "Los Angeles," she replied. "My family just moved to Sweet Valley last week."

"Well, I'm sure you'll find Sweet Valley Middle School a very friendly place."

"I hope so," Maria said, glancing quickly around the room.

Again Jessica had the strange feeling that she knew Maria. She decided to introduce herself after class. Maybe that would clear up the mystery.

As soon as homeroom was over, Jessica grabbed her books and followed Maria to the door.

"Wait up, Jess!" Lila called. "Why are you in such a hurry?"

"I was going to say hi to the new girl," Jessica explained. She glanced at the doorway, but Maria was already gone.

"Since when are you the welcoming committee?" Lila asked.

"It's the duty of the Unicorns to be friendly to new students," Jessica pointed out. "After all, we *are* the most important girls in school."

"Exactly," Lila answered. "So why should we have to be friendly to total strangers?"

Jessica opened her mouth to speak again, but instead she sneezed.

"Are you getting a cold?" Lila asked, moving a few steps away.

"I hope not. Steven has one, and if he gave it to me, I'll kill him." Steven was the twins' fourteen-year-old brother.

"I'm glad I'm an only child," Lila commented. "You're exposed to fewer germs that way."

The two girls eased into the rush of students streaming down the hall. "Didn't you think there was something *interesting* about Maria?" Jessica asked.

"Well, I *did* love her outfit," Lila admitted.

As they turned the corner, Jessica spotted Maria standing in front of a locker. "There she is now. I'm going to say hello."

"Go ahead," Lila replied. "I've got to read those poems Mr. Bowman assigned before English class starts."

Jessica grinned. "I wish thee luck!"

Maria was turning the combination lock around and around. A look of frustration crossed her pretty face.

"Need a hand?" Jessica asked.

Maria looked up in surprise. "I'm sure I have the right combination," she said. "But it refuses to open."

"Let me try," Jessica suggested, handing Maria her books. "What's your combination?"

Maria took a little slip of paper from her purse. "Yep, that's what I thought," she said. "Thirteen, twenty-four, twelve."

Jessica twirled the knob three times and pulled open the locker door.

"Amazing!" Maria marveled. "How did you do that?"

"Years of practice," Jessica joked. "Did you make a complete circle past twenty-four?"

"Oh, *that* explains it," Maria said. She closed the locker door and tried the combination again. This time it opened easily.

"Didn't you have locks on your lockers at your last school?" Jessica asked.

"I—uh, no," Maria stammered. "We sort of had . . . an honor system."

"Wow," Jessica said. "If we didn't have locks, there's no telling what kind of stuff would end up in our lockers—old bananas, dirty gym socks . . ."

Maria laughed, and once again Jessica had the strange feeling they had met before. "By the way, my name is Jessica Wakefield. We're in the same homeroom."

"Do you have a twin sister?" Maria asked.

Jessica nodded. "Elizabeth."

"I *thought* you two looked an awful lot alike!"

"When we were younger we used to dress alike," Jessica said. "Then it was impossible to tell us apart. We used to pretend to be each other and drive our teachers crazy."

Maria laughed as she pulled a social studies book from her locker. "Sounds like fun. I love fooling people like that." She glanced down the nearly deserted hallway. "We'd better get going."

"Where are you headed?" Jessica asked.

Maria opened her notebook, where she had written a list of all her classes and teachers. "Mrs. Arnette," she replied. "Social studies."

"Me, too. Come on, I'll show you the way." Jessica giggled. "You'll just love the Hairnet."

"The Hairnet?" Maria repeated as they headed down the hallway.

"She always wears a hairnet, and she's about three hundred years old," Jessica explained.

"Sounds like my last tutor," Maria said, laughing.

"Tutor?" Jessica asked.

Maria cleared her throat. "I, um, had a tutor for math. I was taking this advanced class, with things like geometry and calculus—"

"You're kidding!" Jessica was impressed. Steven hadn't even taken those courses yet.

"And anyway, I got a little behind," Maria confessed. "The truth is, I *despise* math!"

"Join the club!" Jessica said as the girls turned a corner. "Why did your family move here from Los Angeles, anyway?"

Maria looked away. "Business," she answered quietly.

Jessica wanted to ask more questions, but something in Maria's tone made her hesitate. She paused in front of Mrs. Arnette's room. "You know," she mused, "this may sound crazy, but I'd swear I've seen you somewhere before."

For a moment, Maria's eyes widened, and she seemed startled by Jessica's words. But then she smiled and shook her head. "I've just got one of those faces. A lot of people think I look familiar. But I'm pretty sure we've never met."

Maria slipped into the classroom just as the bell buzzed through the empty hall. Jessica lingered for another moment. *There's something mysterious about that girl*, she told herself. *And I'm going to find out what it is!*

Two

◇

The next morning Jessica sniffled loudly as she sat down at the kitchen table and watched Elizabeth finish her cereal.

"Too bad about your cold," Elizabeth said sympathetically.

Jessica reached into the pocket of her robe for a tissue. She gave Steven a dirty look and blew her nose. "It's Steven's fault."

Steven blew his nose even more loudly. "Hey, don't blame me," he said hoarsely. "Half the freshman class is home with this cold."

"Well, it's not fair," Jessica moaned. "I'll miss the Unicorn meeting this afternoon."

"Not to mention that poetry quiz in English," Elizabeth added, grinning.

Mrs. Wakefield stopped stirring a pitcher of orange juice and gave Jessica a suspicious glance.

"Don't worry, Mom," Elizabeth said quickly. "Jessica would never fake a cold if it meant missing a Unicorn meeting!"

Jessica blew her nose again. "I'm *not* faking!"

"I know, honey," Mrs. Wakefield said, reaching over to pat Jessica on the shoulder.

Elizabeth pushed back her chair and reached for her backpack. "Amy and I are working on a special edition of the *Sixers* this week, Mom," she said as she walked toward the door. "We're doing a write-up about each of the clubs at school for people who might be interested in joining them."

"Sounds like a lot of work," Mrs. Wakefield commented.

Elizabeth nodded. "I'm going to work at Amy's after school, OK?" She smiled at Jessica and Steven. "I wouldn't want Amy to come here and be exposed to all these germs!"

"Just be home in time for dinner," Mrs. Wakefield said.

"I'll get your homework for you, Jess," Elizabeth said.

"Gee, thanks," Jessica muttered as the door slammed behind Elizabeth.

Jessica finished her orange juice and headed listlessly for the family room. It just wasn't fair, catching this cold. Especially when Elizabeth had somehow managed to avoid it. They *were* supposed to be twins, after all.

Jessica found Steven already stretched out on the couch with a blanket around him. "How come you get the couch?" she demanded.

"I have a fever," Steven replied, sniffling. "I'm much sicker than you are."

"In the head, anyway," Jessica mumbled, grabbing the TV remote control off the coffee table.

"Give me that!" Steven cried hoarsely.

Jessica slumped into a chair. "You're way too sick to handle such a big responsibility, Steven."

"Great," Steven growled. "I'll get stuck watching soap operas all day long. What is it you like to watch? *Days of Turnips?*"

"*Turmoil,*" Jessica corrected. "Which we have to watch, because Jake Sommers is fighting for his life after a tragic archery accident."

"How horrible!" Steven cried, pretending to be shocked.

Jessica nodded. "His aunt did it. Well, she's not really Jake's aunt, she's his mother, but of course he doesn't know that."

"Of course."

"Actually, she was aiming for Jake's half brother, Lance."

Steven dove under his blanket. "Enough already!"

"OK, I can take a hint," Jessica muttered. "I'll fill you in later." She began flipping through the channels.

"How about *Wrestlerama*?" Steven suggested.

"No way. I am *not* going to watch two sweaty fat guys throw each other around."

"I had a lot more fun when I was sick all by myself," Steven said testily.

Jessica flipped to a movie that was just starting. "How about this?"

"What is it?"

Jessica looked in the newspaper. " '*The Visitor*,' " she read. " 'An alien from outer space befriends a young girl.' " She looked over at Steven. "It's a few years old, but it's better than *Wrestlerama*."

"Oh, all right," Steven agreed reluctantly. "I'm too weak to argue."

"I brought some more juice, you two." Mrs. Wakefield entered, carrying two big glasses. "You both need to drink lots of fluids."

"Thanks, Mom," Jessica said, reaching for one of the glasses.

"If you need me, I'll be working in the living room." Mrs. Wakefield worked part-time as an interior designer. Since Steven and Jessica were sick, she was working at home.

Jessica turned her attention back to the movie. Three young kids were riding their bikes up a hill when they came upon a strange, eerie light behind a tree.

"I'll bet you that's the spaceship," Steven murmured.

"Shh," Jessica hissed.

She took a sip of her juice and watched as the three children jumped off their bikes and headed toward the strange light. As they stepped nearer, there was a closeup of their frightened faces.

Suddenly Jessica leapt out of her chair, spilling juice down the front of her robe. "That's *her!*" she cried. "I can't believe it!"

"Quiet!" Steven snapped. "The alien's coming!"

Jessica knelt in front of the television screen, waiting for another closeup of the children. Finally she nodded excitedly.

"That's Maria!" she cried. "Maria Slater. I'm positive." She pointed to the girl on the screen and turned to face Steven. "I just met this girl yesterday!"

"Sure you did."

"I'm serious, Steven. I helped her open her locker."

"Why would a movie star like her be hanging around with you?" Steven asked.

Jessica sat back on the carpet, recalling her brief conversation with Maria. Why hadn't she revealed her true identity? And what *was* she doing in Sweet Valley, anyway?

She gazed thoughtfully at the little girl on the TV screen. Now she knew why Maria had seemed so familiar. Jessica had seen her in other movies and in commercials, too.

"This explains why she said she had a tutor. And why she didn't know how to open a locker. She probably grew up doing her schoolwork on movie sets," Jessica mused. "I wonder how old she was when she made this movie?"

"Who? The alien?"

"No, *Maria*."

Steven shrugged. "I don't know. She looks seven or eight."

It was hard to tell, Jessica thought. Maria was so much taller now, and instead of the cute little dimpled face, she looked more—well, like a normal, pretty girl.

"But why didn't she tell me who she was?" Jessica wondered aloud.

"She probably didn't want you and your friends bugging her to introduce you to all her movie-star friends," Steven pointed out.

Jessica's eyes lit up with a sudden inspiration. Steven was right! Think of the possibilities! Maria probably knew all kinds of famous people—stars such as Kent Kellerman, Jake Sommers, and who knew who else?

Jessica had already been nice to Maria, without even knowing she was a star. In fact, she was probably Maria'a closest friend at Sweet Valley Middle School!

For the time being, she would keep Maria's secret. Maria must have her reasons, and Jessica wanted to make sure she and Maria stayed friends.

"Thank goodness you gave me this cold, Steven Wakefield," Jessica said. "Or I would never have been home to see this movie."

Steven sneezed. "Glad I could be of help. This movie's pretty crummy, though. You can tell the alien's fake."

Jessica smiled. So what if the alien was fake? She had just found herself a real, live movie star!

"Are you sure you feel well enough to go back to school?" Mrs. Wakefield asked anxiously the next morning. She pressed her palm to Jessica's forehead. "Steven's staying home another day."

Jessica took a last bite of toast. "He just wants to watch *Days of Turmoil*," she replied. "Besides, I feel great, Mom. Really."

Mr. Wakefield stepped into the kitchen. "How's that cold, Jess?" he asked as he poured himself a cup of coffee. "And where's Elizabeth this morning?"

"She left early to work on a *Sixers* project, and I feel much better!" Jessica couldn't wait to get to school and see Maria.

"Take a sweater," Mrs. Wakefield advised.

Jessica dashed upstairs and returned with a purple cardigan just as Steven came into the kitchen, coughing.

"Be sure to tell me what happens with Jake's archery wound," Jessica told him. She grinned at her mother. "Steven just loves *Days of Turmoil!*"

Jessica wanted to talk to Maria during homeroom, but Lila insisted on telling Jessica everything that had happened while she had been absent. There was no way Jessica could spend any time with Maria while Lila was carrying on about the obnoxious new square-dancing unit they were starting in gym class.

Still, Jessica was able to watch Maria while Lila droned on. There was no doubt that she was the girl in the movie. As the credits had rolled by at the end of the movie, Jessica had watched carefully for Maria's name. *Maria Slater*, it had said, plain as day.

But there was nothing in Maria's attitude that would make anyone think *famous star*. Of course she dressed stylishly, but so did Jessica.

Jessica finally caught up with Maria after

English class. She and Elizabeth walked out of Mr. Bowman's class alongside Maria. "Can you believe all this dumb poetry we're doing?" Jessica moaned. "Reading poems is bad enough, but three whole weeks of writing them, too? It's so boring!"

Maria smiled, and Jessica was immediately reminded of the little Maria she had seen in the movie the day before. Same dimples, same grin. Definite star material. *Now* it was obvious.

"To tell you the truth, I'm kind of looking forward to it," Maria answered. "I like to write."

Jessica stared at Maria in disbelief. "You're kidding."

Maria looked away, obviously embarrassed.

"Don't mind Jessica. *Her* favorite class is lunch," Elizabeth said. "You know, if you like to write, we could really use some help on the *Sixers*."

"The *Sixers*?" Maria repeated.

"It's just the sixth-grade newspaper," Jessica cut in. "You've probably got more important things to do with your spare time."

"Well, no," Maria replied, glancing from Jessica to Elizabeth. "I'd love to help out."

Jessica felt her mouth drop open. Why would a famous actress want to write articles for a puny little paper such as the *Sixers*? Maria could be hanging out with Hollywood stars, doing whatever it was that stars did. *Glamorous* things, such as signing autographs or buying fabulous clothes.

"We're working on a big issue this week profiling all the clubs at school," Elizabeth said. "Maybe you'd like to work on one of them."

"I'd *love* to," Maria replied enthusiastically.

"Let's see." The girls stopped while Elizabeth consulted a list in her notebook. "We still haven't assigned stories on the chess club, the drama club, or the Spanish club."

"The drama club," Maria responded instantly. "That would be perfect!"

"Perfect," Jessica repeated, secretly smiling.

"The bell's about to ring. I'll talk to you later about the article, OK?"

"Thanks, Elizabeth!" Maria said, beaming.

Great, Jessica thought as she watched her twin dash off. *Elizabeth is already trying to steal* my *friend away*. She flashed Maria a brilliant smile. "Maria? Would you like to come over to my house after school?" she asked. "We have a swimming pool." Jessica figured that stars loved to lounge around swimming pools. "And don't worry about not having a bathing suit with you. You could borrow one of mine."

"That sounds like fun," Maria said excitedly.

Great, Jessica thought. Yet at the same time she wondered why Maria had accepted her invitation. Shouldn't she have had something more important to do, such as signing contracts for a big movie deal? It just didn't make any sense!

Three

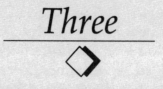

"Swing your partners, do-si-do!" Lila cried later that day, just before gym class. She grabbed Jessica's arm and pulled her across the shiny gym floor.

"Cut it out, Lila," Jessica growled.

"I'm just trying to get you in the mood for square dancing," Lila replied.

"I'll *never* be in the mood for square dancing!"

"Maybe it will be fun," Elizabeth said, joining the group.

Maria walked up to the girls, smiling shyly.

"Hi, Maria," Jessica said brightly. "Too bad you didn't transfer here a little later. You could have avoided square dancing."

"I square-danced once, in a—" Maria hesitated for a moment, "another school I went to. It was fun."

"Howdy, partners! Everyone ready to boogie?" Mandy Miller was doing her best to sound like a cowboy.

"Mandy, have you met Maria Slater yet?" Elizabeth asked as Mandy joined the group. "She just moved here from Los Angeles."

"Nice to meet you," Mandy said cheerfully. "You know, you look kind of familiar."

Maria looked down at her sneakers.

"But what do I know? I can never remember faces, anyway," Mandy continued. "You're lucky you got here just in time for the big square-dancing unit. I hear Ms. Langberg's going to videotape us dancing and send the tape to MTV!"

"I can't wait," Maria said, laughing.

"If you need a partner for square dancing, I'd be happy to volunteer my services," Mandy said.

"Great," Maria replied.

Jessica grimaced. Already Maria was making so many new friends that Jessica wasn't going to seem so special to her, after all. She wondered whether anyone else had caught on to Maria's secret.

"Mandy, are you still planning to try out for the drama club?" Elizabeth asked.

"Yep." Mandy nodded. "There's going to be an introductory meeting tomorrow afternoon."

"That would be a perfect chance for you to

find out more about the drama club for your article, Maria," Elizabeth said.

"Why don't you meet me after school and we'll go together?" Mandy suggested.

"That would be wonderful," Maria replied.

"Maybe I can even talk you into trying out, too," Mandy added.

"Are you interested in acting, Maria?" Jessica cut in.

"I guess everybody thinks about being an actor at some point," Maria replied evenly.

"I was meant to be on stage," Mandy said with a dramatic flourish of her hand. "It's in my blood. My grandparents were vaudevillians. They had this great song-and-dance act, so they moved to California to try to make it big in the movies."

"Were they in any movies?" Lila asked, suddenly more interested.

"Nope." Mandy shook her head. "That's why *I* have to carry on the family tradition!"

"It's hard to make it in Hollywood," Maria said softly.

Jessica watched Maria's face. She thought she saw a hint of sadness in her expression.

"Have you ever acted before?" Maria asked Mandy.

"Jessica and I gave a stunning performance in

the Hairnet's class. We did a comedy routine for a social studies project." Mandy grinned at Jessica. "We deserved an Academy Award for that one, didn't we, Jess?"

Ms. Langberg blew her shrill silver whistle before Jessica could answer. "Line up, girls!" she shrieked. "I haven't got all day!"

Jessica hung back for a moment as the other girls raced to get in line. Why hadn't Maria told everyone about her acting just then? It would have been the perfect opportunity. Instead, Maria's expression had hardly changed when the subject of Hollywood came up. Jessica would have been autographing sneakers and passing out photos of herself if *she* had been the famous actress.

"Here's your lemonade," Jessica said to Maria as she settled next to her on a lounge chair in the Wakefields' backyard that afternoon.

"Thanks," Maria said, accepting the tall glass.

"Sorry about not being able to swim," Jessica said apologetically. "My mom won't let me go in since I just had a cold."

"That's OK," Maria said. "I like just sitting here. It's so peaceful." She gazed around the yard. "This is a beautiful house, Jessica. You're so lucky to have grown up in Sweet Valley."

"I guess," Jessica agreed. "But it's not nearly

as exciting as Los Angeles." She eyed Maria carefully. "Did you ever get to see any famous stars?"

Maria took a sip of her drink. "Um, no, not really." She reached for her backpack. "I guess we might as well get started on our homework. That writing assignment Mr. Bowman gave us is going to take a lot of time."

"Homework?" Jessica widened her eyes in disbelief. "You just got here!"

Maria pulled out her notebook and a pen. "What did you want to do?" she asked.

"Well, I don't know," Jessica said sulkily. "*Talk*, I guess."

"About what?"

"Oh, guys, clothes . . . important stuff."

Maria shrugged. "I guess I'm out of practice at this sort of thing."

"What do you mean?"

"Well, at my last . . . school, I didn't have any close friends." She looked a bit wistful. Then she shook her head, as if she were trying to get rid of an unpleasant memory. "So, what do you want to talk about?"

For the next few minutes Jessica tried to engage Maria in conversation. She brought up all the things she and the other Unicorns spent endless hours on the phone discussing. But somehow Maria didn't seem very interested.

Jessica was almost relieved when Elizabeth stepped onto the patio. She was tired of doing all the talking. "Where've you been?" she asked.

"Amy and I were discussing the *Sixers* club issue with Mr. Bowman." She turned to Maria. "He's our advisor. I told him you were joining the paper and he was happy to hear that." Elizabeth dropped her backpack and sat down next to Maria. "If you've got a few minutes, we could talk some more about the drama club article now."

Maria's dark eyes lit up. "Great!" She reached for her notebook. "I've already written a few notes. You know, questions I can ask when I interview members of the club, that sort of thing."

Jessica made a show of yawning, patting her hand over her mouth. "Can't this wait, Elizabeth?" she asked. "School just ended half an hour ago. Give the girl a break!"

"But I *want* to talk about it!" Maria responded. "I love to write."

"Me, too," Elizabeth said.

Jessica rolled her eyes and groaned. Why was Maria acting this way? She could pass for a first-class nerd!

"What I love most about writing stories is the way you can make up your own world," Maria told Elizabeth. "You can be anyone you want to be. You can do anything you want to do."

"I love to read for the same reason," Elizabeth agreed.

While Maria and Elizabeth were talking, Jessica closed her eyes and leaned back in her lounge chair. Nothing was turning out the way she had imagined. *She* was supposed to be Maria's new best friend, but it was obvious that Maria had a lot more in common with Elizabeth.

"I can't wait to see my name in print!" Maria said to Elizabeth.

"It *is* pretty exciting," Elizabeth answered, smiling.

Not as exciting as seeing your name on a movie screen, Jessica thought in frustration. She couldn't understand why Maria was so excited about the *Sixers*!

Maria stood up to leave just as Jessica opened her eyes. "Thanks for having me over, Jessica."

"Anytime," Jessica replied, feeling almost relieved.

"Come on, Maria. I'll walk you to the door," Elizabeth said. "I'm going over to Amy's to work some more, Jess. I'm having dinner over there, too. Mom already knows."

When Maria and Elizabeth were gone, Jessica ran to the phone in the kitchen, feeling the need for some *real* conversation. She called four different Unicorns, and every line was busy.

"They're probably all talking to each other," she muttered.

"What's the matter, shrimp? Did your finger get a cramp dialing all those numbers?"

Jessica looked up to see Steven peering into the refrigerator. "You must be better," she commented. "You're back to your old obnoxious self."

"Guess what?" Steven said as he browsed. "Jake Sommers's arrow wound wasn't his aunt's fault. It was Lance who did it!"

"I *knew* you'd watch *Days of Turmoil!*" Jessica smiled with satisfaction and headed back out to the patio to get her books. With none of the Unicorns to talk to and Elizabeth gone, she might as well break down and do homework.

As she picked up her backpack, Jessica was surprised to see Maria'a red backpack underneath one of the lounge chairs.

She picked it up and peered inside, wondering what she should do. She wanted to call Maria and tell her she'd left it, but since the Slater family was so new in town, their phone number probably wasn't listed yet.

Jessica reached into the bag and pulled out Maria's English book. Maybe Maria had written her phone number inside. She looked inside the cover, but didn't see a phone number.

Jessica hesitated for a moment. There were a

red notebook and a blue notebook left in the bag. Glancing at them for a phone number would hardly be snooping. After all, she was just trying to be helpful.

The blue notebook was divided into sections for each of Maria's classes. It was neat and organized, but there was no phone number there either.

Jessica checked the first page of the red notebook. Under Maria's name was her address and phone number. Jessica started to close the notebook. Then, feeling a momentary pang of guilt, she turned the page instead. Maria's careful handwriting filled every line.

Jessica glanced at the first few words. *It's the role of my dreams,* she read. *A chance to play the average, all-American, suburban kid. To be what I've always wanted to be.*

Jessica dropped into the lounge chair, the notebook in her lap. This had to be Maria's diary!

She chewed on her bottom lip. She really shouldn't be reading something so personal. But after all, she already knew about Maria's past.

Jessica's eyes dropped to the page in her lap. Again she began to read.

Every good actor knows you have to research a role thoroughly. And there's only one way

I can do that. I'll have to live the life of my character, an average twelve-year-old kid. I'll go to a suburb, attend school, and make friends with the kids. It's the only way. After all, I know absolutely nothing about that life. I grew up in front of the camera, on movie sets, in the public eye. I grew up in a make-believe world.

Jessica shook her head, marveling at the words she had just read. Now it all made sense. Maria was in Sweet Valley to research a movie role!

She turned the page and kept reading.

Of course, no one can know my identity. If people find out who I really am, they won't treat me like one of the crowd. I must act like an undercover agent, forgetting who I really am. For a brief moment in my life, I will stop being a star. I will just be me.

Jessica couldn't believe her amazing luck. There was no doubt about it. She had befriended a movie star!

For the time being, Jessica wouldn't let on that she knew. Maria clearly wanted this kept a secret. And when Maria wanted to tell her, Jessica was sure that she would. But in the meantime, Jessica was going to act like the perfect average twelve-year-old.

With the notebook in hand, Jessica raced up to her bedroom. It was important to plan what she would wear the next day. A star would be watching!

Four

◊

Maria ran up the steps to the front porch of her family's new two-story house. She paused for a moment and gazed at the numbers by the door.

"Two-thirty-six Sierra Avenue," she murmured. She had lived here a whole week, but somehow it was hard to think of this house as home. Still, it *was* her home now, wasn't it? Her home, her school, her town. She even had some new friends. Things weren't going so badly, after all.

Inside, Mrs. Slater was talking on the phone in the kitchen. She waved to Maria, then pointed to a plate of cookies on the kitchen table.

Maria grabbed one and gave her mother a kiss. She dashed upstairs to her sister's bedroom.

Nina, who was sixteen, was sprawled on her bed reading her history book. There were half-empty cardboard boxes spread around the room, and the walls were still bare.

"When are you going to hang up your posters?" Maria asked, leaping onto Nina's bed.

Nina smiled and closed her book. "I was waiting for the assistance of my favorite sister."

"I'm your *only* sister. Aren't you going to ask me how my day went?"

"Actually, I was afraid to ask," Nina admitted. "You've been so anxious about school these past few days, I was preparing to give you my wise-big-sister speech."

"Which one is that?"

"The one where I tell you how it's going to take a while to get the hang of being a normal kid."

"But today I really felt like a normal kid," Maria replied happily.

"Mom said you called to tell her you were going over to a friend's house after school."

"Two friends. Jessica and Elizabeth. They're identical twins, although they're actually pretty different." Maria lay back on the bed. "You're really going to like them, Nina. Especially Elizabeth. We're a lot alike. We both love to read mysteries, and we both like to write. I may even show Elizabeth the story I've been working on."

Nina grinned. "That's great, Maria."

"Elizabeth asked me to help out with the *Sixers*—that's the sixth-grade newspaper. I'm actually going to write an article for them! Can you believe it? I've only been at school a few days!"

"How about the other twin?" Nina asked. "Jessica?"

"She's nice, too. Very friendly. She's a member of the Unicorns."

"Unicorns?"

"They're the most popular girls at school. I should be flattered that Jessica's paying so much attention to me," Maria mused as she kicked off her shoes.

"You don't think she recognized you, do you?" Nina asked.

Maria sighed. "I'm not sure. I don't think so, though. And I can usually tell right away."

"It's bound to happen sooner or later, Maria." Nina's voice was gentle.

"Maybe not." Maria thrust out her chin. "I want them to like me for who I really am. And so far they do."

"You may be right," Nina agreed at last. "After all, you haven't worked since that Princess Macaroni ad. And that was almost two years ago."

"Thanks for reminding me!" Maria grabbed a pillow and tossed it playfully at her sister.

"But look at all you've accomplished!" Nina said. "You started in the business when you were only three. Since then you've made major motion pictures, TV movies, and lots of commercials."

Maria shrugged. "*Made.* Notice you're talking about it in the past," she said sullenly.

"How many kids your age can make the same claim?"

"I know, I know," Maria muttered. "I couldn't go on being a cute little girl forever."

"But you *are* cute!" Nina protested.

"No I'm not." Maria jumped off the bed and stared forlornly into the full-length mirror on the back of Nina's door. "I'm skinny and gangly and about ten feet taller than any of the guys at school. Nobody will ever hire me again as an actor."

"Trust me. It's only a stage. You've just lost all that baby fat you used to have. I went through the same thing, and didn't I turn out OK?"

Maria spun around. "You turned out great!" she said. "And you're a terrific sister, too. A lot of sisters might have resented all the attention I got when I was little."

Nina laughed. "I did, sometimes. There were times when I swore you were the world's biggest brat. But all big sisters think that occasionally. It goes with the territory."

"Remember this?" Maria asked, spotting a

framed photo in one of the boxes. "You and me on the set of *The Visitor*."

"With that boy in his alien costume," Nina added.

Maria nodded. " 'To Maria and Nina—you're both out of this world. And so am I! Best wishes, Henry the Alien.' " She returned the picture to the carton. "Do me a favor, OK? Don't hang any mementos like that on the wall. I want to put all that behind me now."

"Whatever you say." Nina was silent for a moment. "You know, Maria, you can always study acting in college. Your career could start up all over again."

"Actually, I haven't given up on acting entirely," Maria confessed. "That article I'm going to write for the school paper is about the drama club. I met this great girl named Mandy who's going to try out for the club, and I thought, well, maybe . . ."

"Go for it!" Nina cried. "With your experience, you'll star in every play!"

Maria sat down on the edge of the bed. "You know, I think I'm going to like being a normal kid."

"No more tutors," Nina pointed out.

"Or obnoxious kid co-stars," Maria added. "Or grouchy directors!"

"I'm glad we're going to be living here in Sweet Valley permanently," Nina agreed. "I love the high school, although they do give a lot of homework!"

"Homework!" Maria cried. She looked around frantically. "My backpack! I must have left it at the Wakefields' house!"

"Can you do your homework without it?"

"Most of it," Maria said, relaxing a bit. "I'll call Jessica and make sure that's where I left it."

"Will you help me put up a couple of posters first? These blank walls are sort of depressing."

"Where do we start?" Maria asked, hands on hips.

"With this," Nina said, grinning. "I know you said no mementos, but somehow I think this captures the *real* you, Maria."

Maria frowned. "What is it?"

Nina revealed the photo. It showed Maria, age seven and a half, wearing a giant toilet paper roll. "My sister," Nina said proudly. "In her finest *role*!"

Maria giggled. "If you *dare* show that to anyone, I'll tell Mom you kissed Henry when you visited the set of *The Visitor*!" She grabbed for the photo, but Nina snatched it away in the nick of time. "Besides," Maria added, "I think those

Softee ads were some of my finest work. I was a *very* convincing toilet paper roll!"

The phone rang, and a few seconds later Mrs. Slater called from the foot of the stairs, "Telephone, Maria!"

"My first phone call since we moved to Sweet Valley!" she said, and ran to the telephone in the kitchen.

"It's Jessica Wakefield," Mrs. Slater said as she handed Maria the phone.

"Hi, Jessica!" Maria said as she put the receiver to her ear. "Did I leave my backpack over there, by any chance?"

"That's why I'm calling," Jessica said. "Do you want me to drop it off at your house?" she asked eagerly. "I could come by right after dinner. I'm sure my mom wouldn't mind driving me."

"That's OK. I don't really need it."

"But it's no trouble," Jessica insisted. "It's the least I can do for . . . for a new friend."

"Jessica, it's OK," Maria repeated. It was hard to put her finger on it, but Maria felt there was something strange about Jessica's tone of voice. She sounded a bit too—well, *enthusiastic*.

"I could read you your notes or something," Jessica offered.

"That's really nice of you, but—"

"I've got them right here in front of me."

Maria laughed. "Why don't you just meet me a little early tomorrow before school? That way, I'll have time to look over my notes in case there's anything I need."

"Sure," Jessica exclaimed. "That would be great!" She paused for a moment. "So, what are you going to do tonight?"

Maria sat down in a kitchen chair. "Probably just study."

"Yeah," Jessica said. "*I* understand. Just your basic, average evening. Me, too. I'll just eat dinner and do my homework, like your typical sixth grader."

"Whatever you say. I'll meet you on the bench near the flagpole tomorrow morning, OK?"

"I can't wait!"

Maria hung up the phone and sighed. The Wakefields might be twins, but she definitely preferred Elizabeth.

Jessica seemed a little weird.

Jessica arrived at school the next morning a half-hour early. She positioned herself on the bench Maria had mentioned and excitedly scanned the groups of kids for Maria. Now that she knew Maria was working under cover, Jessica couldn't wait to talk to her new friend—even if Maria *was* a bit eccentric. In fact, Jessica was so excited that she felt she would have a hard time keeping her mouth shut about Maria's secret. But, she knew it was better to let Maria tell her about her movie research. That way, she wouldn't have to admit that she had snooped in Maria's notebook.

"Hi, Jessica. Have you been waiting long?" Maria asked, settling next to Jessica on the bench.

"Just a few minutes." Jessica reached behind the bench. "Here's your backpack, safe and sound. I took very good care of it."

Maria laughed. "It's not like there's anything valuable in it. Unless you count my English book. Anyway, thanks."

"Anytime. I'm always glad to help a friend. Just the way your average kid at Sweet Valley Middle School would." Jessica flashed Maria a winning smile.

Maria looked a little puzzled, but then she smiled back. "Kids here are really friendly. Much nicer than others I've known."

Jessica studied the nails of her right hand. "How long do you think you'll stay here?" she asked casually.

"Stay?" Maria repeated. "Well, forever, I hope."

Jessica smothered a smile. *Sure, Maria,* she thought to herself.

"There's so much I want to know about Sweet Valley," Maria continued.

Here they come, Jessica thought. *The research questions.* "Such as?" she prompted.

"Well, where do you guys go shopping, for instance?" Maria asked.

"The mall, mostly," Jessica replied. "Of course, it's probably not as glamorous as what you're used to."

"What do you mean?" Maria asked, a little edgily.

"I only mean, well . . . you're from Los Angeles," Jessica said quickly.

Maria smiled. "They have malls in Los Angeles, you know. In fact, I pretty much lived at the mall near my old house in L.A.!"

"So what else do you want to know? Ask me anything. Think of me as your personal tour guide to the world of Sweet Valley."

"Let's see. I have so many questions. . . . Where do you guys hang out? What do you do for fun? Who's your favorite teacher? What's your favorite subject?"

As Maria spun out her list of questions, Jessica's eyes sparkled with excitement. "This is so amazing!" she cried. "You're very thorough, aren't you?"

"What?" Maria looked confused.

"I mean, I've always heard you guys did stuff like this, but I never dreamed it would be right here in Sweet Valley!" Jessica blurted, unable to hold back the secret any longer.

Maria's features hardened. "Wait a minute. What 'stuff' are you talking about, Jessica? You're not making any sense!"

Jessica shook her head. "You are *so* convincing, Maria! You're going to play a normal kid perfectly!"

A sudden look of understanding passed over Maria's face. She closed her eyes. "Normal?" she whispered.

For a moment, Jessica almost regretted opening her mouth. But she'd come this far. It was too late to turn back. "I know about the movie, Maria," she admitted. "I looked in your backpack for your phone number and, well . . . I didn't mean to, but I couldn't help glancing at your diary."

Five

◈

Maria opened her eyes and stared at Jessica in disbelief. "You read my notebook?"

"I—I didn't mean to," Jessica stammered. "I was looking for your phone number, and your notebook just sort of fell open . . ."

Maria took a deep, steadying breath. What was she supposed to do now?

"I know I shouldn't have looked," Jessica continued quickly, "but after I figured out who you were, I was so curious about why you were keeping it a secret—"

"When did you recognize me?" Maria asked softly.

"When I stayed home from school on Tuesday, Steven and I watched *The Visitor* on TV, and as soon as I saw that cute little girl I knew it was you. Then, when I read your journal and realized you were here to research a movie, everything made perfect sense."

"Perfect sense," Maria repeated dryly. So Jessica had read the story she'd made up and thought it was real. She shot an angry look at Jessica. "You know, you shouldn't have looked in my notebook."

"I know that." Jessica hung her head. "But I promise that your secret is safe with me."

Maria crossed her arms over her chest. Was this the reason Jessica had been so quick to befriend her? Because she thought Maria was here to make a movie? And what about Elizabeth? Was all that stuff about the *Sixers* just an excuse to get to know a star? It was just as it had always been. No one cared about *her*—they cared about a movie star. And if they knew the truth, would she have any friends at all?

"Does Elizabeth know about this?" Maria demanded.

"No!" Jessica assured her. "She's been so busy with the *Sixers* that I've hardly seen her."

Maria rubbed her eyes. A few minutes before she had been perfectly happy, and now everything was ruined. If she told the truth, would Jessica still be interested in her? In any case, Maria vowed to get back at Jessica. *If she wants a star, I may as well give her one!* Maria thought angrily.

"Maria?" Jessica asked anxiously. "Promise you're not angry?"

Maria pursed her lips. "I promise I won't be angry if you promise not to tell a soul about this."

"Oh, you can count on me," Jessica replied earnestly. She tossed her hair over her shoulder. "You know, I'm kind of an actress myself."

"You are?"

"I starred in a production of *The Kite* at the Sweet Valley Community Theater," Jessica said proudly. "Dolores Dufay was my co-star."

"I'm impressed," Maria said. "So as a fellow actress, you will understand that I can't do my research if everyone knows who I am."

"Of course," Jessica agreed excitedly. "I won't tell a soul. Now *I* have some questions for *you*. What's it like to be famous? Do you know lots of stars? Do you know Johnny Buck?"

Maria stared at Jessica in amazement. One minute Jessica had been a nice, normal friend, and the next she was just another adoring fan. Maria felt like she had created a monster. But this was what Jessica wanted, after all. A star. Not a friend. "Uh, sure I know him," she responded.

"What is he like?" Jessica pressed excitedly.

Maria waved her hand. "He's just your average guy, once you get to know him," she replied. The truth was, although she had met him briefly at a charity benefit, he was not exactly a close friend. "People are only stars when you don't know them, Jessica. Once you do, you realize they have problems just like everybody else."

"What problems could a rock star like Johnny Buck have?" Jessica asked, sounding amazed.

"Well—" Maria thought for a moment, "he gets lonely on the road. He wishes he had a place to call home, and good friends he could trust."

"Poor Johnny!" Jessica moaned.

"Yes." Maria nodded wistfully. "Poor Johnny."

"Do you think the next time you two get together, you could . . ." Jessica trailed off.

"Introduce you?" Maria finished. "I guess. The thing is, you couldn't treat him like a star, Jessica. He has all the groupies he needs. Do you think you could treat him like a regular person?"

"Of course I could!" Jessica responded. "I'm not the groupie type. Things like stardom don't impress me."

Maria reached for her backpack and stood. "I'm glad to hear it, Jessica," she said, wondering if Jessica noticed the hint of bitterness in her voice.

Probably not, Maria thought with a resigned sigh. She was too good an actress.

*   *   *

All day, Maria walked around in a daze. At lunch, Jessica invited her to sit at the Unicorner, the Unicorns' regular lunch table. But fortunately, Elizabeth had asked her to sit with her and Amy. At least Elizabeth still seemed to be treating her like a normal human being. She didn't show any signs of knowing about Maria's past. In fact, she was much more interested in talking about writing, and for a while, at least, Maria was able to forget her problem.

The day wore on slowly. After school, Maria met Mandy in front of Mr. Drew's classroom for the drama club meeting. Jessica passed by just as the two girls were heading in the door.

"Are you going to join the drama club, Maria?" Jessica asked innocently.

"No, Jessica," Maria said shortly. "You *know* I'm just here to get information for my drama club article." She had pretty much given up on the idea of trying out for the club now that Jessica knew who she was.

"Well, I was just thinking that if you *did* try out, you'd probably be a natural actress," Jessica said with a sly smile. "I'll bet you've got a lot of talent!"

"I'll talk Maria into trying out," Mandy said confidently. "I refuse to make a fool of myself all alone!"

"I'd stay to keep you company, but I've got Boosters practice," Jessica said.

"Boosters?" Maria asked.

"The middle-school cheering squad," Mandy explained.

"You'll have to come watch us sometime," Jessica said meaningfully. "You might find it useful."

Maria cast a warning glance at Jessica. She hoped her message was clear. "See you, Jessica," she said evenly.

"Have fun!" Jessica called as she ran off down the hall.

"Why would watching the Boosters be *useful?*" Mandy asked as the girls entered Mr. Drew's classroom.

"Who knows?" Maria shrugged. She settled into an empty seat and motioned for Mandy to join her. There were already about fifteen other students in the room. "I like your outfit," Maria commented, anxious to change the subject.

Mandy was wearing baggy pants with black suspenders. She had a man's paisley tie knotted loosely around her neck. "Thanks," she said.

"Where do you buy your clothes?"

"A very chic little boutique called the Clothes Closet," Mandy answered with a laugh. "Actually, it's a second-hand store. You'd be surprised what you can find there." She pulled at the waistband of her pants with a resigned smile. "Of course, these pants weren't always quite so baggy. I bought them before I was sick."

"Sick?"

"I had cancer," Mandy explained matter-of-factly. "But I'm better now. Pretty soon I'll have my real hair back."

"You mean that's not . . . *you*?" Maria asked, staring in surprise at Mandy's chin-length dark brown hair.

"Nope. It's genuine fake hair," Mandy replied. "My real hair fell out when I had radiation treatments. It was all the way down to my waist." She shrugged. "But I'm going to grow it back to that length—you just wait and see."

Maria didn't know what to say. She had never met anyone who'd had cancer. Once in a TV movie she'd played a girl who had it, but that was hardly the same thing. In the movie, Maria had been very brave. But she had always wondered if she would be that brave in real life. Now here was Mandy, living through something Maria had only pretended to understand.

Before she could say anything, Mr. Drew swooped into the room. "Welcome, future drama club members!" He was a small, wiry man with longish, curly red hair. "I'm Mr. Drew, the club sponsor, and I'm delighted to see so many students interested in the noble profession of acting." He surveyed the room, smiling broadly. "How many of you have acted before?"

A few kids raised their hands, including Mandy. "I did that social studies project with Jessica," she whispered. "That counts, doesn't it?"

Maria nodded. It was all she could do to keep her hand down. After all, she was a professional actress. Instead, she took out her notebook and pen and began to take notes for her *Sixers* article.

"Only four people?" Mr. Drew shook his head. "*Wrong*. We're *all* actors, every day of our lives. How about that time you tried to convince your teacher that your pet iguana ate your math book? Wasn't that acting?"

Everyone laughed. Maria wrote very quickly, trying to make sure she was quoting Mr. Drew accurately.

"Or that birthday when you told your Aunt Gertrude you *loved* the zebra-striped sweater she bought you?" Mr. Drew continued. "You've been acting all your lives!" He sat down on the edge of his desk. "But real acting, good acting, is hard work. It requires practice and dedication and skill. And that's what I'm going to try to teach you."

Maria smiled to herself, recalling the long hours of work she had endured over the years. The memorizing. The endless rehearsing. Mr. Drew was absolutely right.

"The drama club puts on several productions during the year. I'd like you each to audition with a short reading so that I can determine who will be actors and who will work behind the scenes on lighting or set design."

Mandy cast a nervous glance at Maria.

"It doesn't have to be elaborate. It can be anything you choose. Drama, comedy, even Shakespeare if you're feeling brave. Just a few minutes will give me an idea of how you handle yourself on stage."

A girl in the front row raised her hand. "Can we try out with someone else?"

"Sure!" Mr. Drew exclaimed. "But if you can't find someone to try out with, I'd be happy to read any role you require. Of course, I won't be on stage with you. I'll just sit in the audience and read the lines."

Mandy raised her hand. "When are the tryouts?"

"A week from tomorrow, after school. And remember, even if you aren't selected as an actor, there is a lot more to theater besides acting."

As other students asked questions, Maria

stopped taking notes and gazed out the window. She had almost forgotten how much she loved the excitement of acting. It all came back to her in a rush. It was in her blood, and it wasn't fair that she had to give it all up because she was no longer a cute and cuddly seven-year-old.

She wondered what it would be like to be on stage. Despite all her movies and commercials, Maria had never actually performed before a live audience. Before a director and a crew, sure. But she had never had the thrill of listening to a live audience applaud her performance.

"So, what do you think?" Mandy asked when the meeting finally ended.

"Oh, I should have plenty of information for my article," Maria answered as they got up.

"No, I mean, will you try out?" Mandy asked.

Maria headed for the door. "I—I couldn't," she stammered. She imagined the look on Jessica's face when she heard Maria was trying out for the drama club. *Then* how long would Jessica be able to stay quiet?

"Come on," Mandy insisted. "You're not going to let me make a complete idiot of myself all alone, are you? I need moral support, Maria."

"The truth is, I can't act," Maria said, marveling at the words as soon as she had uttered them.

"You heard Mr. Drew—everybody acts. And

how will you know if you're any good unless you try out?"

Maria paused, nibbling on her thumbnail. How much worse could things get?

"Come on, Maria," Mandy urged. "It'll be a lot more fun with a friend."

Maria looked at Mandy and sighed. She could really use a friend right now herself. "OK," she said at last. "What have I got to lose?"

Six

◇

Near the end of Boosters practice, Jessica stood on the sideline of the football field and threw her baton high into the air. She reached to grab it, but the silver baton fell to the ground with a thud.

"That does it," Janet Howell cried. "Let's quit practicing for today. *Some* of us just aren't concentrating!" Janet, an eighth grader, was the president of the Unicorn Club. All of the members of the Boosters were also Unicorns, with the exception of Amy Sutton.

Jessica knew she was the "some of us" Janet was referring to, but she didn't really care. All day she had been thinking about Maria's secret movie research. Keeping a secret *that* big was not easy—especially for Jessica, who wasn't exactly known for keeping her mouth shut. It just wasn't her nature. Maria was asking the nearly impossible. Still, Jessica had gone for an entire day without spilling the beans.

Jessica picked up her baton and cast Janet a mysterious smile. "Some of us have more important things on our minds than Boosters practice."

The girls began walking across the field. "Like what?" Janet asked.

"Yeah," Lila added. "You've had a smirk on your face all day. What gives?"

Jessica shrugged nonchalantly. "It's privileged information." She glanced at the others, then shook her head regretfully. "I don't think I can trust you guys with a secret that's this important."

"Let me guess," Amy said sarcastically. "It has something to do with Bruce Patman."

"No." Jessica crossed her arms over her chest.

"Jake Hamilton?"

"Nope."

Amy tapped her sneaker on the grass. "Aaron Dallas, then?"

Jessica smiled at the mention of Aaron's name. Everyone had been green with envy when he had taken Jessica on a date to a Lakers basketball game.

"Not even Aaron," Jessica replied.

"Well, whoever it's about, I'm sure it won't be a secret for long," Amy remarked.

"Yes it will!" Jessica protested. "My lips are sealed!"

Amy rolled her eyes. "Anyway, I've got work to do on the *Sixers*. See you all later!"

Jessica watched as Amy ran off across the field. Now there were only Unicorns left, people she could trust.

"Well?" Lila prompted. "Are you going to tell us, or do we have to guess?"

"Great idea!" Jessica cried. "Why don't you all try to guess?" That way, she couldn't really be accused of telling Maria's secret—and Amy would be proven wrong.

"At least give us a hint," Janet said, sounding annoyed. "I don't have all day."

"Let's see," Jessica murmured. "It involves all of us. And it's very exciting."

"We're going on a class trip," Lila suggested. "To Europe!"

"Dream on, Lila," Jessica said. "Besides, this is even more exciting."

"Someone famous is coming to visit," Tamara Chase, an eighth grader, shouted.

Jessica smiled. "You're getting warmer."

"I'll bet it's Johnny Buck!" Grace Oliver cut in. "Johnny Buck is coming to play at a school assembly."

"Oh, come on," Janet said irritably.

"You never know," Jessica hinted. "Certain

stars might be interested in Sweet Valley Middle School."

"So he *is* coming?" Ellen Riteman screeched. "Johnny Buck is coming *here?*"

"No, no. That's not what I said." Jessica groaned. This guessing game was going nowhere fast. Maybe she should just come right out with it. This could take all night.

Jessica took a deep breath. "Look. I'm going to tell you the secret. But you have to promise *never* to tell a soul. And if you do tell, you'll be immediately expelled from the Unicorns."

The girls fell silent, exchanging uneasy glances.

"OK," Janet said at last. "We promise. But this had better be good, Jessica."

"It's better than good. It's incredible," Jessica insisted. "You know Maria Slater?"

"The new girl?" Ellen asked.

Jessica nodded. "Did anyone notice anything, well, *unusual* about Maria? Did she seem vaguely familiar to anybody?"

No one spoke.

"I'll give you a little hint," Jessica said. " 'Princess Macaroni—it's fit for a queen!' " she sang off key.

Lila snapped her fingers. "The Princess Macaroni girl!" she cried. "That was Maria!"

"I *knew* she looked familiar," Ellen said.

"Remember that toilet paper ad?" Tamara

Chase asked. "The one where the girl was dressed up like a giant toilet paper roll?"

Jessica nodded. "That was Maria. And she's been in a ton of movies."

"*The Visitor*!" Janet cried. "Wasn't that little girl Maria?"

"Yep," Jessica confirmed. "And remember the TV movie from a couple of years ago where the girl had cancer? That was her, too."

"This is amazing," Ellen marveled. "We have a real star right in our own school, and we didn't even know it! Why didn't we recognize her?"

"She's changed a lot," Jessica said. "I didn't recognize her, either, until I saw *The Visitor* that day I stayed home from school."

"If we'd known who Maria is, we would have paid more attention to her," Janet pouted.

"Why didn't she tell us?" Lila demanded.

"That's the best part of all." Jessica was grinning from ear to ear. This was the moment she had been waiting for. She motioned for the other Unicorns to come closer.

"Maria is here *under cover*," Jessica whispered.

"You mean she's a spy?" Ellen asked.

"In a way. She's researching a role for a new movie. It's about kids in a suburban middle school. Kids like *us*." Jessica gazed at her audience triumphantly.

"Maria's making a movie about *us*?" Ellen cried.

"Well, I don't know if it's about us *exactly*. But she's here at school to find out what an average twelve-year-old is really like."

"We're average!" Tamara exclaimed.

"Tamara's right," Janet said. "We're perfectly average, *and* the most popular girls in school. Who could be better for Maria to use as her models?"

"This means if we get close to Maria, she might introduce us to all kinds of famous people," Ellen pointed out.

"Johnny is a good friend of hers," Jessica said casually.

"Johnny Buck?" Ellen and Tamara screamed at the same time.

"Shh," Jessica warned, glancing furtively over her shoulder. "Someone might hear you!"

"Jessica's right," Janet agreed. "We've got to keep this top secret." She smiled at Jessica. "You did the right thing telling us, Jess. Unicorns have to share these things."

Jessica smiled happily, basking in Janet's praise.

"But if word gets out about Maria's movie, her research will be impossible. She may have to move to another school," Janet continued.

"Good point, Janet," Grace agreed. "We can't let Maria know that we know what she's up to."

"We'll have to treat Maria like a regular person, even though she's a star," Jessica reminded the group. "That's what I've been doing."

"OK, everybody remember: not a word of this to anyone!" Janet said. "We have to keep this a secret."

Jessica began walking across the field with the others, who were chattering excitedly. She hoped they could be trusted. After all, keeping a secret could be exhausting.

As soon as Maria got home from the drama club meeting, she said a quick hello to her mother and dashed up the stairs to her room.

She closed her bedroom door and collapsed onto her bed with a heavy sigh. A few seconds later, there was a knock at her door.

"Maria? Can I come in?" Nina opened the door and peered into the room. "How was your drama club meeting?"

"Great," Maria said truthfully. "I'm definitely going to try out."

"I'm so glad. I think it'll be a wonderful way for you to meet people."

"In fact, I'm going to write up my notes on the meeting while it's still fresh in my mind," Maria said.

"OK," Nina said. "I've got a ton of homework to do, anyway."

As Maria watched her sister close the door, a feeling of dread washed over her. She desperately wanted to tell Nina about the disastrous day she'd had. But she could not quite bring herself to admit what she had told Jessica that morning. Nina would be so disappointed in her if she knew that Maria had let Jessica believe she was still a movie star.

Things were only going to get worse now. Jessica would undoubtedly tell all her friends, and they would tell all their friends. . . . Before she knew it, the entire student body of Sweet Valley Middle School would know about Maria Slater, the undercover actress.

For a brief moment, Maria considered picking up the phone and calling Jessica to tell her the truth. She tried to imagine what she would say. *Hello, Jessica? That diary you read was really just a short story. It was just fiction, not fact. There is no research, there is no movie, and I am just a has-been actress trying to pretend she's a normal kid.*

No way—she just couldn't do it. It would be so humiliating, and besides, she couldn't risk it. She wanted to fit in, she wanted to be liked, and Jessica was one of the few friends she had.

Of course, she had Elizabeth and Mandy, too. At least she *hoped* she did. Maria rolled over on her bed and wiped away a stray tear with the back of her hand. She thought about the casual way Mandy had told her about her cancer. Maria really admired her new friend's courage. And she knew that her problems hardly compared to Mandy's ordeal.

Maria took a deep breath and reached for her notebook. She was tired of feeling sorry for herself. Besides, she had an article to write.

Seven

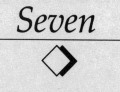

At noon on Friday, Maria stepped cautiously into the lunchroom.

"Maria! Come sit with us!" Elizabeth called, motioning to the empty seat next to her.

Maria glanced around nervously, then darted toward the table where Amy and Elizabeth were sitting.

"Is something wrong?" Amy asked.

"Wrong? No," Maria said quickly. She slid into the chair next to Elizabeth. "It's just that this girl—I think her name is Ellen—has been following me around all morning."

Amy pointed with her fork to the lunchroom entrance. "Is that her?"

Maria snuck a glance at the door. "That's her, all right," she answered, sinking lower into her chair.

"That's Ellen Riteman," Elizabeth informed Maria. "She's one of the Unicorns."

Maria opened her lunch bag and pulled out a sandwich wrapped in plastic. "I'm sure she's just trying to be nice."

"Maybe," Amy said doubtfully. "But don't count on it. When a Unicorn seems nice, she's almost always up to something."

"Amy, that's not *always* true." Elizabeth smiled at Maria. "*Usually* true, but not always."

"Look out," Amy warned under her breath. "Here come two of them now."

Jessica and Janet were approaching the table, with wide smiles plastered on their faces.

"Maria!" Jessica called. "Don't you want to sit at the Unicorner?"

"Please, Maria," Janet chimed in. "We saved a seat just for you."

"Thanks," Maria said quietly. "But I'm fine right here."

"I just thought you should come over to our table for a *typical* Sweet Valley Middle School lunch," Janet said.

"They're serving mystery meat today, Maria," Jessica added.

Maria bit her lower lip. A *typical* lunch, Janet had said. It was just what Maria had feared. Jessica had told the Unicorns her secret. They had been fawning all over her that day. At first Maria had tried to fool herself into believing that they were just being nice because she was new. But they hadn't been this friendly earlier in the week.

Anyway, she knew all the signs. This wasn't how friends acted. This was how *fans* acted. She was getting the star treatment.

Maria looked Jessica straight in the eye. "I think I'll pass on the mystery meat," she said coolly. "I need to talk to Elizabeth about my *Sixers* article."

Jessica smiled at Janet. "Sure, Maria," she said meaningfully. "We understand."

"See you later," Janet added.

The two girls headed back to the Unicorner, giggling.

"What was *that* all about?" Elizabeth asked as she watched her twin depart.

"Don't let them get to you, Maria," Amy advised. "All the Unicorns have a screw loose. It's a membership requirement."

Maria concentrated on opening a carton of milk. Part of her desperately wanted to tell Elizabeth and Amy what had happened, but she just couldn't bring herself to admit it. It was too humiliating.

"You know," Amy mused, "the Unicorns were acting especially weird after Boosters practice yesterday afternoon." She shook her head. "I hope it's not catching."

"Weird?" Elizabeth asked as she reached for one of Amy's potato chips. "How?"

"Well, Jessica claimed to know the world's most important secret, and you could tell she was dying to let everyone in on it."

"Jessica hasn't told me anything," Elizabeth said. "It's probably just the usual Unicorn gossip."

Maria looked down at her lap. Hot tears welled up in her eyes. She breathed deeply, willing herself not to cry. It was a trick she had learned as an actress—she could turn her tears on or off at will. But today it was harder than usual.

"Maria? Are you OK?" Elizabeth asked, sounding concerned.

Maria cleared her throat. "I'm fine." She reached for her backpack and pulled out her notebook. "Would you like to see what I've done on that drama club article so far? I wrote a rough draft when I got home from the meeting yesterday."

"How was the meeting, anyway?" Amy asked while Elizabeth began to read Maria's article.

"Great. Mr. Drew is wonderful." Maria took a sip of milk. "Mandy even talked me into trying out!"

"I think I'd have stage fright," Amy said. "Have you ever acted before?"

Maria hesitated for a moment. She really didn't want to lie to Amy. She'd already lied to too many people. "Mr. Drew says we're all actors, whether we know it or not," she answered at last.

Elizabeth looked up from the notebook. "Maria, this article is fantastic! If this is just your rough draft, I can't wait to see the finished product. You're really a talented writer."

Maria smiled, glowing at Elizabeth's praise. It felt good to be appreciated for something *real*. "Do you really like it?" she asked shyly.

"We may even use this as our lead article," Elizabeth replied. "Have you written anything else I could read? I'd love to see some more of your work."

"I've been working on a short story," Maria said hesitantly. "But I'm not done with it yet. And I'm not sure it's really any good. . . ." She trailed off, remembering the *last* time someone had looked at her story.

Elizabeth took a bite of her sandwich. "If it's anything like that article, I'm sure it's great."

Slowly Maria reached into her backpack and

retrieved her red notebook. She really did want to hear Elizabeth's opinion. What harm could it do to let her read the story? She opened to the first page and handed the notebook to Elizabeth.

"It's the role of my dreams," Elizabeth read aloud. She looked up and smiled at Maria. "Good opening."

"May I read it too?" Amy asked.

"Be my guest," Maria replied.

Amy moved next to Elizabeth and the two girls began reading silently. Maria nervously took a bite of her sandwich. What if they didn't like the story? She had never shown her writing to anyone except Nina. Jessica had seen it—but that was an accident.

"This is incredible!" Elizabeth said when she had finished.

"I loved it, too!" Amy agreed. "What a great idea for a plot! How did you think of it?"

"I just thought it might be interesting. Of course, I never write stories about my own life," she added. "I save that for my journal at home. It's locked in my desk drawer."

"That's what I do, too," Elizabeth said. "Except my desk drawer doesn't lock. Sometimes I wish it did—not that I can't trust Jessica, but . . ."

"But you can't trust Jessica!" Amy finished, laughing.

Maria smiled bitterly. She knew all about not trusting Jessica.

"So how is this story going to end?" Elizabeth asked.

"I don't know," Maria admitted.

"Well, I can't wait to find out what happens!" Elizabeth said.

Maria smiled in spite of herself. "Me either."

After lunch, Elizabeth and Amy dropped Maria off at her locker.

"Thanks for the great work on the article," Elizabeth said. "Looks like the *Sixers* may have a new star reporter."

A star reporter, Maria repeated to herself as she watched Elizabeth and Amy head down the hallway. Now, *that* was the kind of star she wanted to be!

It took two tries, but Maria finally managed to open her locker. As she rummaged through her books, she was startled to find a small box wrapped in purple tissue paper. There was a note attached. *For Maria*, it read. *Welcome to Sweet Valley Middle School. The Unicorns.*

Maria stared at the little box. How could the Unicorns have gotten into her locker? Then she remembered her first day at school, when Jessica had helped her open her locker. She must have remembered the combination!

Maria ripped off the tissue paper and glanced inside the box. Under a layer of soft cotton was a thin purple bracelet. It was pretty, and obviously expensive.

Suddenly a strange memory came back to her. She couldn't have been more than seven or eight years old. A young fan named Karen had sent her a solid gold charm bracelet in the mail, and Maria's mother had made her return it with a nice thank-you letter. "Gifts like that are only meaningful when they are exchanged by people who really care about each other," Mrs. Slater had told Maria.

Now Maria thought she understood what her mother had meant. The Unicorns hadn't given her the bracelet because they cared about her. They had given it to her because they thought she was a movie star.

"I think you all know why I called this emergency Unicorn meeting," Janet said that afternoon after school. She glanced at the girls who had assembled in her bedroom. The room was buzzing with conversation and, as usual, everyone was wearing something purple.

"I don't know," Belinda Layton said as she entered Janet's bedroom, stepping carefully over other Unicorns sprawled on the carpet.

"Me, either," Mandy said breathlessly as she

popped through the bedroom door. "Sorry I'm late, guys. I got tied up talking to Maria Slater about the drama club tryouts."

"That's what this meeting's about!" Lila exclaimed.

"The drama club?" Mandy asked in disbelief.

"No, *Maria!*" Lila cried.

"Are we going to invite her to join the Unicorns?" Mandy asked. "That would be great!"

"I suppose we could make Maria an honorary Unicorn while she's here," Jessica said. "It would be great for her research—"

"Wait a minute," Mandy interrupted. "What do you mean, while she's here? Maria just moved here! I'm sure she'll be in Sweet Valley for a long time."

"We'd better start at the beginning, for those of you who weren't at yesterday's Booster practice," Janet said importantly. "Order, everyone."

The Unicorns kept right on talking.

"I said *quiet!*" Janet screamed at the top of her lungs.

Suddenly the room fell silent.

"That's more like it," Janet said primly. "As I was saying, for those of you who haven't heard the biggest news in the history of the Unicorns, Maria Slater is visiting our school under cover."

"Under *what?*" Mandy demanded.

"She's not really a student, Mandy," Jessica explained patiently. "She's just pretending to be one so she can see what the life of a typical twelve-year-old is like."

"Why would she need to know that?" Mandy demanded. "She already *is* a typical twelve-year-old!"

Janet shook her head. "Do the words *Softee Toilet Paper* mean anything to you?"

Mandy put her hands on her hips. "I know it's hard to believe, Janet, but I don't spend a whole lot of time thinking about toilet paper."

"How about Princess Macaroni?" Jessica offered.

"I don't think much about macaroni, either." While the other Unicorns giggled, Mandy looked helplessly at Belinda for assistance. Suddenly, at the very same moment, both girls screamed.

"That's Maria!" Mandy cried. "How could I have been so stupid? I *knew* she looked familiar!"

"She's changed a lot since her big movie roles," Janet pointed out.

"All that time at the drama club meeting, she never said a word about her past," Mandy marveled.

"You haven't heard the best part yet," Janet continued. "She's here to do research for a brand-new movie. And she's using *us* as her subjects.

So far, the Unicorns are the only people who know her secret."

"*I* discovered it," Jessica said proudly.

"But why didn't she tell me?" Mandy wondered aloud, her brow creased. "I thought we were friends."

"I'm sure she *wanted* to tell you, Mandy," Jessica replied. "But if everyone at school finds out, it might ruin her research."

Mandy considered that for a moment. At last she nodded her head. "I suppose you're right." She brightened a bit. "Do you think she'd give me some pointers for my acting tryout?"

"I want her to introduce me to some big producers in Hollywood so *I* can be discovered," Lila interjected. "I'm thinking about asking my dad to take me to Paris to find the right dress. You can't be discovered in *jeans*, after all."

"I'm going to make friends with Johnny Buck," Jessica added importantly. "Maria says he's very lonely."

"You and the Buck?" Ellen sneered. "Dream on, Jess!"

"Just wait and see," Jessica replied frostily. "After all, I *am* Maria's closest friend."

"But if we can't tell Maria we know about her, how are we going to get her do all this stuff?" Janet asked. "What's the point of knowing a star if you have to pretend she's just like everybody else?"

For a few moments, all the Unicorns were silent. Janet had brought up a very good point.

"We've got to tell Maria we know," Lila said at last. "But we've got to be subtle."

"It would be better if Maria admitted the story herself," Jessica reasoned. "Otherwise she'll think I told you guys."

"You *did* tell us," Lila pointed out.

"But Maria doesn't have to know that," Jessica argued.

"I've got it!" Janet cried, leaping up. "Truth or Dare! We'll get Maria to play Truth or Dare, and when it's her turn, we'll force her to admit she's an undercover actress!"

"That's brilliant, Janet!" Lila exclaimed. "But you only play Truth or Dare at sleepovers."

"So we'll have a sleepover!" Janet answered. "Right here, tonight. It is Friday, after all. I'm sure it will be OK with my mom."

"It's perfect!" Jessica agreed. "Maria will have to tell us the truth, and we can all pretend to be surprised. All in favor, raise your hands!"

Mandy was the only one who didn't raise her hand.

"Mandy?" Janet asked, sounding annoyed. "Don't you like this idea?"

"Sure," she said quietly. "I like it. I was just thinking that only yesterday, I was treating Maria like a normal kid. I can't believe she fooled me so completely!"

"She's an *actress*, Mandy," Jessica replied. "It's her job to fool people!"

Eight

"Mom, may I go to a sleepover tonight at Janet's?" Jessica asked as she burst through the front door of the Wakefields' house later that afternoon.

Mrs. Wakefield was watering a large fern in the living room. "Isn't this awfully sudden?" she asked, setting down her watering can.

"Janet invited us at the Unicorn meeting this afternoon," Jessica explained. "And it's OK with her mom."

"How many girls are going?"

"All the Unicorns. Plus Maria Slater, the new girl you met Wednesday. We called and invited her during the meeting."

"That was sweet of you," Mrs. Wakefield said, smiling. "It's going to be awfully lonely here tonight without you, Jess. Steven's going to a football game, Elizabeth is having dinner at Amy's, and you'll be over at Janet's." She threw up her hands. "How will your father and I *ever* stand the quiet?"

"You'll manage. Too bad Elizabeth isn't home. I wanted to tell her about our meeting, but I guess it'll have to wait until tomorrow." Jessica ran toward the stairway. "I'm going to pack. Will dinner be ready soon?"

"Why are you in such a hurry?"

"This is going to be a big night, Mom," Jessica replied seriously. "A very big night!"

Maria reached for another handful of popcorn and settled onto the floor in Janet's bedroom. She was surprised at what a good time she was having—especially since she almost hadn't come.

When Jessica had called that afternoon to invite her to a Unicorn sleepover, Maria's first instinct had been to say no. She knew why they wanted her there—and it *wasn't* because they really liked her. It was the same reason they had given her the bracelet—because of who they thought she was.

But after several minutes of Jessica's pleading, Maria had finally given in. Now she was glad she had. The Unicorns had been treating her wonderfully. No one had asked her anything about her past, and Maria had begun to wonder if she was wrong about Jessica. Maybe she *had* kept her mouth shut, after all. Perhaps all the friendliness was just a coincidence.

"Now that we've eaten enough junk food to make us completely sick, what do you want to do?" Janet asked the group.

"We could tell ghost stories," Ellen suggested.

"Wait!" Jessica cried, casting a glance at Maria. "I've got a better idea. Let's play Truth or Dare!"

"Does everybody know how to play?" Janet asked.

Fortunately, Maria had once played Truth or Dare in a TV mystery movie called *Mansion of Blood*. She was relieved she wouldn't have to ask the others what the rules were.

"Everybody get in a circle," Janet instructed.

"But I'm not finished braiding Lila's hair!" Ellen whined.

Lila shook out the tight French braid Ellen had been working on. "This is more *important*, Ellen."

"Oh," Ellen said. "I forgot."

While the Unicorns formed a circle on the floor, Janet turned off all the lights except one. "For atmosphere," she explained.

Janet settled next to Jessica on the carpet. "I'll start," she said excitedly. "Let's see. Who should I begin with?" She surveyed the circle of girls watching her expectantly. "Jessica!" she decided.

Jessica nodded. "Truth," she said calmly.

"Wait a minute!" Janet scolded. "I'm supposed to ask you truth or dare first!"

Jessica rolled her eyes. "So ask already," she said impatiently.

Janet cleared her throat. "Truth or dare?"

"She *told* you, Janet," Ellen interrupted. "She chooses truth."

Janet paused to glare at Ellen. "All right then, Jess, here's your question. And don't forget that you *must* answer it truthfully!"

"I know the rules, Janet."

"Did you or didn't you kiss Aaron Dallas when you two went out on your date?"

While the rest of the group laughed, Jessica smiled serenely. "I hate to disappoint all of you," she said when the noise had died down, "but the answer is no. Not that Aaron didn't want to. I'm *sure* he did. But he was a perfect gentleman."

No one seemed very interested in Jessica's answer. "Who's next?" Lila prompted immediately. "Let's do another one."

"It's Jessica's turn," Janet said.

All eyes were on Jessica as she looked around the circle. "This one is for—" she paused, and her gaze landed on Maria, "Maria!"

A hush fell over the group, and Maria realized that all eyes were glued on her.

"Truth or dare, Maria?" Jessica asked.

Maria swallowed hard. As long as Jessica didn't ask anything too personal, choosing to answer a question would be easier than picking a dare. Besides, in *Mansion of Blood* she had chosen a dare, and as a result she had nearly gotten killed by a maniac living in the attic.

"I choose truth," Maria replied.

Jessica studied the ceiling for a few moments while she composed a question.

"Hurry up, Jessica!" Lila urged.

"OK, I'm ready," Jessica said at last. "Remember—you have to tell the truth, Maria," she added seriously.

Something about Jessica's tone made Maria very uncomfortable. Suddenly she had a sinking feeling that she knew what Jessica was going to ask.

"The question is: are you, or are you not, a famous actress in hiding?"

The room was perfectly still. Maria stared at Jessica, debating whether or not to yell at her for betraying their secret. But in truth, she wasn't really surprised. The amazing thing was that Jessica hadn't spilled the beans sooner. *Oh well*, she thought to herself, *I might as well play this part for all it's worth.*

"I have to tell the truth?" Maria asked.

"*Yes!*" several of the Unicorns yelled at once.

"Well, in that case . . ." Maria paused, looking at each girl in the circle. She knew that in drama, timing is everything. "The answer is yes!"

For a moment, nobody spoke. The mouths of all the Unicorns dropped open. Then, as if on cue, all the girls burst into screams.

"I *knew* I recognized you!" Ellen cried.

"You were the Princess Macaroni girl, weren't you?" Belinda asked.

For the next few minutes Maria basked in all the attention. It was like having her own private fan club. She hadn't had this much praise heaped on her since she was a little girl, and she had to admit it was fun. Before long, Maria was talking about her undercover research. And the more she talked, the more her imagination took over. It was like improvisational acting—she just made things up as she went along.

"It's going to be hard to keep this quiet, Maria," Janet said seriously. "But you can count on us."

"Don't worry about it," Maria said with a wave of her hand. Just then, all her anxiety about the movie story seemed silly.

"Who else will be in the movie, Maria?" Lila prodded. She handed Maria the soda she had asked for and settled next to her on the bed.

"The parts haven't all been cast yet," Maria told the group. "But we know for sure that Johnny will be in it. And Melody Power, Kent Kellerman, and Nick England will have small speaking parts," Maria added, spinning the story as she went along. She had forgotten herself and fallen completely into her character, just like the professional actress that she was.

"This is so incredibly amazing!" Ellen whispered.

"I can't believe you really know these people," Mandy murmured.

Maria grinned. "You get used to working with stars after a while," she said casually. "They're just regular people."

"Kent Kellerman is *not* a regular person!" Tamara exclaimed, putting her hand over her heart. "He's the most adorable guy on the planet!"

"Yeah, I guess he is kind of cute," Maria conceded. "Anyway, you can see for yourselves. You're all invited to the movie set when we start filming, and I promise to introduce you to everybody."

The girls began screeching so loudly that Mrs. Howell stuck her head in the door. "Could you keep it down to a dull roar in here?" she asked. "It's awfully late, girls."

"Sorry, Mom," Janet replied.

"Maria, do you think we could watch the actors actually working?" Mandy asked quietly when Mrs. Howell had left.

"Sure," Maria replied. "Maybe you can pick up some acting pointers, Mandy."

"Maybe *I* can pick up some *actors*," Janet said with a giggle.

For the rest of the night, all the Unicorns could talk about was Maria's movie. By the time everyone had crawled into their sleeping bags to go to sleep, even Maria was getting tired of the topic.

She was lying in the dark with her eyes open when Jessica crawled over to her. "Maria?" she whispered. "You're not mad, are you?"

"Mad?"

"About my asking you that question during Truth or Dare."

Maria let out a long breath. "No, Jessica," she said at last. "The story was bound to come out eventually."

"I knew you'd say that. Besides, isn't it kind of a relief to have your secret out in the open?" Jessica asked. "I *hate* keeping secrets!"

So I've noticed, Maria thought as she watched Jessica crawl back to her sleeping bag.

Next to her, Maria heard Mandy stir. "Maria?" Mandy whispered, turning onto her side.

"Yes?"

"How come you didn't tell me about all this after the drama club meeting?" Mandy whispered.

"I—I couldn't," Maria said softly. "You understand, don't you, Mandy? I wanted to tell you more than anyone."

"Sure," Mandy answered. "I understand. Are you still going to try out with me for the drama club?"

"If you want me to."

"Are you kidding? How can I lose with you for an acting coach?" Mandy replied. She rolled onto her back. " 'Night, Maria."

" 'Night," Maria whispered, but she knew she wouldn't be falling asleep anytime soon. The excitement had worn off, and reality had set in. A terrible feeling of dread overcame her. What had she done? How could she possibly have told so many lies? She'd had the perfect opportunity to tell everyone the truth, and what had she done? *Lied.*

Somehow, at the time, it had felt more like acting than lying. She had gotten caught up in playing the role of a star, and she hadn't wanted to disappoint her audience. But when they found out the truth, her "audience" was going to be very disappointed.

Nine

◇

"Lizzie! Have I got news for you!"

Jessica dashed across the Wakefields' front lawn, carrying her sleeping bag in one hand and her overnight bag in the other.

Elizabeth was on her knees, pulling weeds out of the flower garden. "You're just in time to help me," Elizabeth told her twin. She wiped her forehead with the back of her hand. "Steven's in the back mowing, and Mom wants you and me to pull these weeds."

"In a minute," Jessica said impatiently. She dropped her sleeping bag onto the grass and sat down on top of it. "First, I've got major news to tell you. It seems like I haven't seen you in ages. Are you finally done with that stupid *Sixers* issue?"

"Almost," Elizabeth replied. "And it's not stupid, Jess. It's going to be one of our best issues."

"I didn't mean it that way. It's just that you've been so busy this week, and I haven't had a chance to really talk to you." She rubbed her hands together. "Wait until you hear about Maria!"

Elizabeth tossed aside a dandelion. "I *knew* there was something going on with the Unicorns and Maria," she said. "Ever since I saw you and Janet fawning all over her at lunch yesterday, I've been meaning to ask what you were up to. Amy said you were acting strangely at Boosters practice, too."

"There's a good reason, Elizabeth. Maria is a star! A famous actress! When she was younger, she made zillions of movies and commercials."

"So that explains it," Elizabeth said. "I've always thought there was something familiar about Maria's face. Why didn't she tell anybody?"

"Because she's here under cover!" Jessica replied. "She doing research for a new movie, and she wanted to see what typical suburban twelve-year-olds are really like. She's researching *us*, Elizabeth! Isn't that fantastic?"

Elizabeth didn't answer. Instead, she chewed on a blade of grass, frowning. She remembered the story Maria had shown her. This sounded awfully familiar. Why had Maria specifically said that she didn't write stories about her own life? There was definitely something strange going on, Elizabeth decided.

"Don't you get it, Elizabeth?" Jessica cried in frustration. "We're going to be famous, sort of!"

"I just feel a little strange about this," Elizabeth admitted. "I wish Maria had told me."

"But she couldn't!" Jessica said, throwing up her hands in frustration.

"I guess you're right," Elizabeth agreed. "So how did you first find out Maria was an actress?"

"I saw one of her old movies on TV that day I stayed home from school."

"Why didn't you tell me right away?" Elizabeth asked.

Jessica shifted uncomfortably on her sleeping bag. "The thing is, Maria didn't want anyone to know who she really is, so I had to keep it secret. Until last night, anyway, at Janet's sleepover. She finally decided it would be OK to tell everyone about the movie."

"Who's going to be in the movie?" Elizabeth asked.

"Everyone who's anyone!" Jessica exclaimed. "Kent Kellerman, Melody Power, Johnny Buck Nick England—"

"All of them?" Elizabeth interrupted. "In the same movie? Sounds too good to be true."

"Amazing, isn't it? And the best part of all is that Maria's invited us to visit her on the set and meet all her co-stars!"

Elizabeth smiled to herself, imagining poor Maria at Janet's sleepover, surrounded by adoring Unicorns. Now that she knew about Maria's real identity, she promised herself she would continue to be Maria's friend—not her fan.

Maria probably had enough of *those* already.

After lunch on Monday, Maria was surrounded by a crowd of kids at her locker. Things like this had been happening all day, ever since the news had spread about her big movie. At first all the attention had been exciting, but she was beginning to get awfully tired of signing autographs and answering the same questions again and again.

"Maria, do you have a minute to talk?"

Maria finished signing an autograph for a seventh-grade boy and looked up to see Elizabeth standing next to her. "Sure," she said, "if I can ever get out of here!"

"Do you *really* know Nick England?" an eighth-grade girl demanded.

"Would you autograph my notebook?" another girl asked plaintively.

"Um, maybe later," Maria said, casting a helpless look at Elizabeth.

Elizabeth reached for Maria's elbow. "Come on," she said forcefully. "There's an emergency phone call for you, Maria. I think it's from Hollywood."

The crowd parted, and Elizabeth and Maria made a mad dash for the safety of the library.

"Elizabeth, you saved my life!" Maria said breathlessly as they fell into chairs at a table in the corner.

"Word sure travels fast around here, doesn't it?" Elizabeth exclaimed.

"All this attention's pretty silly," Maria said a little sheepishly. "After all, I'm the same person I was last Friday. I guess you've heard all the details by now."

Elizabeth nodded. "To tell you the truth, I felt a little hurt when I first found out," she admitted. "But I understand why you were trying to keep things a secret."

"I finally gave up on that," Maria replied. "I knew it was just a matter of time before everyone figured out who I was, anyway."

"I just want you to know that I really like having you for a friend, Maria. And it's not because you're a famous actress. It's because, well, I think you and I are a lot alike." Elizabeth smiled. "Anyway, I don't care if you're only going to be here a short time. I hope we can still be good friends."

"Me, too," Maria said softly. She looked away, debating what to say next. Elizabeth was being so open and honest with her; shouldn't she be honest as well? It would be such a relief to tell someone the truth. And who could she trust more than Elizabeth, who really seemed to like Maria for herself?

"You know, Elizabeth," Maria began haltingly, "there's something I'd really like to tell you."

"What?"

Maria looked Elizabeth squarely in the eye. What was the worst that could happen if she told the truth? Elizabeth would be mad, but she would probably forgive her eventually. "I want you to know how glad I am we've become friends," Maria said slowly. "You're one of the few people who really seems to know me. And—"

"That reminds me," Elizabeth interjected. "I think a lot of kids would like to know you better, Maria. You've had such an interesting life. I know you're working for the *Sixers*, but how would you feel about being interviewed for the paper?"

"An interview?" Maria repeated dully.

"It wouldn't take me long to do, and I think it would make a good story."

Maria sighed. She couldn't even tell Elizabeth the truth. It was too late. "Can we wait a while on the interview, Elizabeth?" she asked. "I'm kind of busy right now. You know—getting unpacked at home, plus memorizing my lines for the movie. I'll let you know when I'm ready."

"Sure," Elizabeth agreed. "Just promise me it's an exclusive, Maria! Don't go giving an interview to a rival school paper!" she added, laughing.

"You have my word," Maria promised. *Whatever that's worth* she thought.

"Uh-oh," Elizabeth murmured, glancing over at a girl who was approaching them.

"What's wrong?" Maria asked.

"That's Pamela McDonald. She's—wait, I'll explain later," Elizabeth whispered.

The girl sat down next to Elizabeth. "Hi, Elizabeth," she said sweetly.

"Hi, Pamela," Elizabeth replied evenly. "Have you met Maria Slater?"

"No, but I've heard about her," Pamela said. "Nice to meet you, Maria."

"Hi," Maria said. She took a deep breath, expecting the usual barrage of questions about her life as a star, but Pamela had turned all her attention back to Elizabeth.

"Could I borrow your English notes from last Friday?" Pamela asked, gazing admiringly at Elizabeth.

"Sure." Elizabeth reached into her notebook and pulled out three sheets of paper.

"You are *so* thoughtful, Elizabeth!" Pamela gushed. She turned to Maria. "Isn't Elizabeth the nicest person you've ever met?"

Maria smiled at Elizabeth, whose cheeks were turning a vivid shade of pink. "No doubt about it," she agreed.

Elizabeth took her social studies book from her backpack and opened it. "I've got a ton of reading to do," she murmured. "How about you, Maria?"

"Me?" Maria asked. One look at Elizabeth's face told her the right answer. "A ton," she agreed. "Maybe even two tons."

Pamela stood. "Well, I guess I'll be going so you can get to your reading. Thanks, Elizabeth. As soon as I've copied your notes I'll return them."

"Take your time," Elizabeth replied.

Pamela gazed at the sheets of paper in her hand. "You have the most beautiful handwriting, Elizabeth!" she exclaimed. "I just *love* the way you dot your *i*'s!" She walked off, shaking her head in wonder.

"How *do* you dot your *i*'s?" Maria whispered when Pamela was out of earshot.

"With a dot," Elizabeth replied. "Like everyone else!" She stared after Pamela. "I hope I didn't seem rude. It's just that she's been following me around lately, and it's sort of embarrassing. I know it sounds crazy."

"Not to me!" Maria said, laughing. "I know all about fans!"

Just then Mandy Miller entered the library. She waved at Elizabeth and Maria, a mischievous grin on her face. "Say, aren't you the Softee Toilet Paper girl?" she asked Maria.

"That was one of my proudest acting moments!" Maria replied, laughing.

"That's why I brought this," Mandy said, reaching into her book bag. She pulled out a foot-long piece of toilet paper. "Would you mind autographing it for me?"

Maria and Elizabeth burst into laughter so loud that Ms. Luster, the librarian, wagged her finger at them in warning.

"You're crazy, Mandy!" Maria whispered. It felt wonderful to be laughing about her past for a change, especially since everyone else was taking it so seriously.

"I saw you being attacked by autograph hounds this morning," Mandy explained. "I thought maybe you could use a laugh." She pointed to the bookshelves. "I'm going to find some plays for us to look at. Maybe we can decide on our readings for the drama club tryouts."

"Great! Mind if I come along?" Maria asked.

"You're the expert!"

While Mandy and Maria headed for the shelves, Elizabeth picked up a magazine on the table and casually thumbed through it. The bell was going to ring soon.

Near the back of the magazine, a large announcement caught her eye. *Essay Contest*, it read.

The deadline is approaching for submissions to our annual essay contest. This year's theme is "Becoming an Individual." Enter soon and you may be our lucky winner!

"Becoming an individual," Elizabeth murmured. It would be an interesting subject to write about—especially from the perspective of a twin. She reached for a pen and jotted down the contest information in her notebook.

She was nearly done when Mandy and Maria returned. Mandy was carrying a thick book of plays.

"Any luck?" Elizabeth asked.

The two girls looked at each other and began to giggle. "We both like *Romeo and Juliet*," Mandy explained, opening her book to the play. "In fact we both want to play Juliet in the balcony scene."

"There's just one little problem, though," Maria added. "We need a Romeo!"

Elizabeth began to laugh, too.

This time Ms. Luster had had enough. She stomped over to their table, looking very annoyed. "What *is* it you girls find so amusing?" she demanded. She glanced at the book Mandy was holding. "*Romeo and Juliet* is a tragedy!" she cried, shaking her head.

"Not without Romeo it isn't," Mandy replied, giggling.

The bell rang, and Ms. Luster pointed toward the door. "Get going, ladies," she instructed. "And please! Next time try to be more quiet in the library!"

Ten

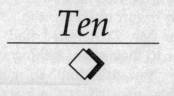

The next morning, Maria had already signed two autographs before she'd even entered the front doors at school. She had just finished signing her third when Mandy joined her on the front steps.

"Was that one of your groupies?" Mandy asked her.

Maria laughed. "Only three autographs this morning," she said. "I'm already old news."

"I spent last night trying to memorize the balcony scene from *Romeo and Juliet,*" Mandy said as the girls entered the crowded lobby.

"Did you learn it?"

"The only thing I learned is that memorizing is hard work! Don't you have any secret acting tips that you can share with me?"

"Practice," Maria advised. "Then practice some more."

"We should get together after school and practice together," Mandy suggested hopefully.

"Good idea!" Maria said. "You can come over to my house if you want."

"Great."

Maria smiled to herself. She was having a friend over to her new house! It wasn't a big deal for other kids, but when was the last time she had been able to invite someone over?

She thought back over the last few crazy years. Then she remembered. The last time she had invited a friend home from school had been when she was nine. The "friend" had been another actor, and her "house" had been a make-believe set. She'd been filming a chocolate-chip-cookie commercial.

"I'm really going to need your help, Maria. I'm having a hard time with Shakespeare," Mandy admitted.

"Don't worry, we're going to be great," Maria said. "The balcony scene is *so* romantic." She stopped in the middle of the hallway, clasping her hands together. " 'Oh Romeo, Romeo! Wherefore art thou Romeo?' "

Several students turned to stare as Mandy broke into applause. "That was terrific, Maria," she said, grinning.

"There's just one little problem," Maria reminded her. "We're still in need of a Romeo."

"Don't forget that Mr. Drew said he'd read the part for us if we couldn't find anyone else to do it."

"But he'd be sitting in the audience reading from the play," Maria argued. "It's just not the same as working with a real, live actor on stage."

"That's why we're going to say hello to Donald Zwerdling," Mandy whispered.

"Zwerdling?" Maria repeated doubtfully.

"Over there." Mandy pointed to a short, red-haired boy standing before an open locker.

"Wasn't he at the drama club meeting?"

"Exactly. You're looking at Mr. Romeo Zwerdling!"

"Romeo? No way!" Maria groaned. "His pants are too short!"

"Look," Mandy said grimly. "We're running out of possibilities. Last night I called every guy I could think of who was at the drama club meeting. Almost every one of them said he'd already decided on a reading. Two still hadn't, but they both said *Romeo and Juliet* was out of the question."

"But it's Shakespeare!"

"*Mushy* Shakespeare," Mandy corrected. "So it's down to Donald Zwerdling. Remember—you said yourself that it's easier to work with a real, live actor."

Maria peered at Donald. "Well, he's breathing, anyway. But can he act?"

"Who cares?" Mandy asked. *"We* can." She grabbed Maria's arm. "Try to sweet talk him. Our theatrical futures may depend on it."

"Oh, Donald!" Mandy called. "Could we talk to you for a minute?"

Donald was paging through a notebook as the two girls closed in. "Sure," he said, looking a little surprised. "What about?"

"Nice notebook," Maria remarked. "It's so very . . . uh, *blue*."

"And clean," Mandy added. "Not a mark on it." She moved a little closer. "Donald," she said sweetly, "are you still planning to try out for the drama club?"

"Yep," Donald said shyly as he shut his locker.

"Have you chosen a reading yet?" Mandy asked eagerly.

Donald smiled proudly. "I already have it memorized. I'm doing the final slipper scene from *Cinderella*."

"Seriously, Donald," Mandy pressed.

"I *am* serious!" Donald exclaimed, sounding offended. "I'm playing Prince Charming."

Maria hid her smile behind her hand.

"Who's playing Cinderella?" Mandy continued.

Donald shrugged. "I couldn't find a Cinderella, so I guess Mr. Drew will do it." Suddenly his eyes lit up. "Say, would one of you want to—"

Maria shook her head firmly. "We're both doing a scene from *Romeo and Juliet*."

"Who's Romeo?"

"It's beginning to look like Mr. Drew," Mandy admitted.

"Well, if either of you change your mind and want to play Cinderella, give me a call. I've got a glass slipper and everything."

Donald strode off down the hall.

"Great. We've got two Juliets and no Romeo. We'd better find one soon or we're going to have to change the name of the play to plain old *Juliet*," Maria joked as they started toward homeroom.

"Maria! Mandy! Wait up!"

The girls turned around to see Jessica and Lila galloping toward them. Lila nearly knocked over a small sixth-grade boy in her haste.

"We have the most incredible news!" Jessica said, panting.

"You mean *I* have the most incredible news," Lila corrected.

Jessica grimaced. "OK," she conceded. "Go ahead."

"It's about my father's yacht," Lila began. She tossed her thick brown hair over her shoulder.

"He's just had it redecorated, and I've convinced him to throw a party for Maria and the cast of her movie!"

"That *is* incredible!" Mandy exclaimed.

Maria swallowed hard. "Incredible," she repeated.

"I thought we'd schedule the party for Saturday, if that's OK with you, Maria," Lila said. "Since you told us the filming is going to start next week, it seemed like the perfect time for you to introduce your co-stars to everyone in Sweet Valley."

"Perfect," Maria murmured.

"Is that all right?" Lila asked anxiously. "I mean, can you get hold of everybody in time?"

"Sure," Maria replied numbly. "I can get hold of them."

"I hope Johnny Buck isn't giving a concert that night," Jessica said. "I was hoping we could spend some time together."

"I wonder if Kent Kellerman could take time out of his filming schedule to stop by school for our tryout and play Romeo?" Mandy asked.

"In your dreams, Mandy!" Jessica said with a laugh.

"Well, if you get Johnny, I get Kent!" Mandy retorted.

"Come on," Lila urged. "We're going to miss

homeroom. We can split up the stars later. Maybe we should flip a coin or something."

Jessica, Mandy, and Lila began walking toward homeroom. "Aren't you coming, Maria?" Mandy called.

Maria shook her head. "I forgot something," she lied. "I'll be there in a minute."

She dashed down the hall to the girls' room. Safely inside, Maria splashed cold water on her face. She stared in disgust at her own reflection. How could this be happening to her? Every day her lies got bigger and bigger, and her world was spiraling out of control.

You fake, she whispered to her reflection. *You've been acting for so long, you've forgotten how to tell the truth*. And now, when she finally wanted to stop acting, no one would let her.

It really didn't matter. She didn't know how to play the part of plain old Maria Slater, anyway.

After school, Mandy came over to Maria's house to practice for their tryouts and brought Elizabeth and Amy along to serve as an audience. Maria wasn't in the mood anymore, but she didn't want to disappoint them.

Mandy and Maria worked on their staging in the living room. The more involved Maria got in the play, the less she thought about her problems.

That was the nice part about acting, she realized. She could forget all her problems for a while and be somebody else.

While Maria and Mandy planned their scene, Amy and Elizabeth ate cookies in the kitchen with Nina and Mrs. Slater.

"Maria's told us a lot about the *Sixers*," Nina said to Elizabeth.

"She's a very talented writer," Elizabeth said. "I hope she continues to work on the paper as long as she's here."

"Here?" Nina asked curiously.

Before Elizabeth could respond, Maria and Mandy burst into the kitchen. "It's showtime!" Mandy announced. "Please follow the usher. She'll seat you in the theater."

Maria gestured toward the living room, where the girls had arranged four chairs at one end of the room. After everyone was seated, she stepped forward.

"I thought you were the usher," Nina teased.

"Now I'm the director," Maria replied. "Could we have quiet on the set, please?" She cleared her throat and waited for the audience to stop giggling. "Ladies and gentlemen—oops, I mean, *ladies*—I am proud to present act two, scene two of *Romeo and Juliet*, by William Shakespeare."

"Maybe we should explain what's happening," Mandy suggested. "Here's the deal. Romeo and Juliet are teenagers. They're in love, but their parents disapprove. So Romeo sneaks over to Juliet's house one night, and she hangs out on her balcony so they can chat. Everybody get it?"

The audience nodded. "Which one of you is Romeo?" Amy inquired.

"We're both Juliet. We haven't found a Romeo yet," Maria explained.

"That's kind of unromantic, isn't it?" Nina teased.

Mandy rolled her eyes. "This audience is very uncooperative," she complained.

"Actors have to ignore distractions," Maria instructed. She stepped into the middle of the living room. "I'll go first. She closed her eyes for a moment, then began to recite her lines:

Oh Romeo, Romeo! Wherefore art thou Romeo?
Deny thy father, and refuse thy name!
Or, if thou wilt not, be but sworn my love,
And I'll no longer be a Capulet.

She stepped back and motioned to Mandy.

"What's a Capulet?" Amy whispered.

"It's Juliet's last name," Maria explained.

"My turn," Mandy said. She took a deep breath and began to speak:

Oh Romeo, Romeo! Wherefore art thou Romeo?
Deny thy father and refuse thy name!

"Wait a minute," Nina murmured to Mrs. Slater. "Am I crazy, or did somebody rewind this movie? We just heard this part!"

"We both want to be Juliet!" Mandy insisted, throwing up her hands, "so we're both practicing our Juliet lines."

"This is never going to work. Maybe we should practice a little more while you guys finish up the cookies," Maria suggested.

"I think we need to recast the audience," Mandy whispered.

Maria smiled. She knew they were just teasing, and besides, there was something reassuring about the way her friends and family were making acting fun this afternoon. She had almost forgotten just how much she enjoyed it.

Eleven

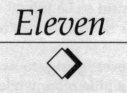

"I hope you don't mind the way we gave you and Mandy a hard time this afternoon," Nina said to Maria that evening.

Maria was sitting on the front-porch steps, watching the stars grow brighter. "Actually, I had a lot of fun this afternoon," she said seriously. She motioned to the top step. "Want to join me?"

"The view's awfully nice," Nina said, settling next to Maria. "The stars are so much brighter here than they are in L.A."

"Stars," Maria muttered. "Am I ever sick of *that* word."

"What's wrong?"

"Nothing," Maria replied quickly.

"Come on. You're a good actress, but you

can't fool me. You've seemed troubled ever since that sleepover. Did something happen that night?"

"Well, I ate too much junk food," Maria tried to joke.

"They've figured out who you are, haven't they?"

Maria gazed at her sister in surprise. "How did you know?"

Nina chuckled. "Sisterly intuition. Plus little things Elizabeth and Mandy said this afternoon." She patted Maria gently on the back. "It was just a matter of time, you know. I'm only surprised it didn't happen sooner."

Maria closed her eyes and fought back the tears threatening to spill down her cheeks. What would happen if she told her sister the whole truth? Wouldn't Nina be furious at her for telling so many lies?

"You know, once the kids at school get used to the fact that you've been an actor, they'll start treating you like a regular person. Just wait and see," Nina advised.

This time Maria couldn't stop the tears. "They'll *never* treat me like a regular person!" she blurted. "Pretty soon they're going to despise me!"

"Maria, what are you talking about?" Nina asked gently. "Don't be silly! Look at all the friends you've already made. Elizabeth and Jessica, Mandy, Amy, the Unicorns—they all like you."

"But you don't know *why* they like me!" Maria cried. She turned away from Nina and buried her head in her hands. "I lied to them, Nina. Once they found out about my past, I couldn't bear to tell them the truth—that I'm just a plain old twelve-year-old, after all. So I told them I was here doing research for a big movie, with lots of famous stars in it. And once I got started, I just couldn't stop the lies. The whole school thinks I'm something I'm not."

"So that's it! Poor Maria," Nina said comfortingly. She put her arm around Maria's slumped shoulders. "Why did you feel you had to lie? You're a wonderful person all on your own! You don't need to tell stories to make people like you."

"It wasn't really my fault," Maria said, sniffling. "It started when Jessica looked in my personal notebook, and she saw that story I was working on about the actress who goes to a school so she can find out what normal kids are like. She thought the story was real, not fiction. Then, during the sleepover, we played Truth or Dare—"

"I'm beginning to get the picture," Nina said, nodding her head. "But you can't really blame Jessica," she added gently.

Maria wiped away a tear. "I know," she

admitted. "I had plenty of chances to tell everyone the truth. But it was fun being the center of attention. I felt like a real star again! And after a while, I couldn't bear to disappoint everyone."

"Don't you mean, disappoint *yourself?*" Nina asked.

Maria nodded. "I just wanted everybody to like me, I guess. But now the Unicorns are planning a big party on Lila's father's yacht for the cast of my new movie. Only there isn't any cast. Or any movie." She gazed up at the sky hopelessly. "What am I going to do now?"

"If you want people to like you for yourself," Nina said slowly, "you're going to have to start *being* yourself."

"You mean tell them the truth?"

"I know it sounds hard, but I think people will be a lot more understanding than you think," Nina said.

"Hard? It sounds *impossible!*"

"Trust me, Maria," Nina insisted. "Friends like Elizabeth and Mandy and Amy aren't going to suddenly stop liking you because you made a mistake."

"That's three people," Maria said grimly. She glanced up at the glittering stars. "But what about the rest of the school?"

*   *   *

"Purple crepe paper," Jessica said firmly. She pounded on the kitchen table with her fist. "It's got to be purple, Lila."

On Wednesday afternoon Jessica, Lila, and Ellen started planning the big yacht party for the cast of Maria's movie. So far the only thing they had agreed on was that Lila could ask for Kent Kellerman's autograph first, since she was the official hostess.

Lila looked across the table at Ellen. "Would you *please* talk some sense into Jessica?" she demanded. "Purple is out of the question."

Ellen took a sip of milk and shrugged. "I agree with Jessica," she said. "After all, the Unicorns are sponsoring this party. Why shouldn't the crepe paper be our official color?"

"Because the Unicorns *aren't* sponsoring the party, my father is!" Lila fumed. "And he just had the entire yacht redecorated in apricot and puce."

"Apricot?" Ellen echoed.

"It's the color of an apricot," Lila snapped. "You know, kind of orange."

"So what's puce?" Jessica demanded.

"It's—" Lila hesitated. "It's the color of a puce."

"A puce?" Jessica repeated. "What's *that*?"

She shrugged. "It's very difficult to describe. Anyway, *you* should know, Jessica. Your mother's an interior designer."

"My mother would never design anything in *puce*," Jessica shot back. She eyed Lila suspiciously. "You don't know what color it is, either, do you, Lila?" She pushed back her chair and stood up.

"Where are you going?" Ellen asked.

"To get the dictionary," Jessica replied. "I'm going to look up *puce*."

A few seconds later she returned. "Listen to this!" she said triumphantly. " '*Puce*'—'a color, usually brownish purple'."

She dropped the dictionary onto the kitchen table. "I rest my case. Purple crepe paper will be perfect!"

"All right, Ms. Know-it-all," Lila growled. "If it means that much to you, we'll have purple crepe paper."

Jessica smiled happily, but Ellen still seemed anxious.

"What's wrong now, Ellen?" Lila demanded.

"Apricot and puce?" Ellen said. "I don't know, Lila. It sounds like a really awful dessert. Maybe your father should have hired Mrs. Wakefield as his decorator."

"How are the party plans coming?" Elizabeth asked later that evening as she set the table for dinner.

"We got nothing accomplished," Jessica complained. "Unless you count the purple crepe paper."

"Unicorn parties always have purple crepe paper," Elizabeth pointed out.

"Try telling that to Lila," Jessica moaned. "She's being even more bossy than usual, since the party's going to be on Mr. Fowler's yacht. You'd think *Lila* was the one who discovered Maria, when it was really me!" Jessica lifted the lid off a saucepan on the stove and inhaled deeply. "This spaghetti sauce smells scrumptious," she said.

"What do you mean, you *discovered* Maria?" Elizabeth asked.

Jessica reached for a spoon and dipped it into the sauce. "Well, I recognized her before anyone else," she said. "And of course, I was the one who found out about her undercover work."

"How *did* you find out about that, anyway?"

As Jessica tasted the spaghetti sauce her face suddenly went pale.

"Jess? What's the matter?" Elizabeth asked. "Too much garlic?"

"No, it's fine," Jessica said quickly, dropping the spoon in the sink. "I've got to go do my homework, Lizzie. The Hairnet gave us tons of reading."

"Wait just a minute, Jessica Wakefield!" Elizabeth cried. "You haven't answered my question. How did you find out about Maria's movie?"

Jessica slumped against the kitchen counter. "Promise you won't lecture me about how sneaky and underhanded and generally rotten I am?"

"That's asking a lot, but OK, I promise," Elizabeth said.

"Remember that day last week when Maria came over after school? Well, she left her backpack behind, and while I was trying to find her phone number so I could call her, I sort of accidentally read her diary." Jessica looked down at the floor, ignoring Elizabeth's gaze.

"Jessica, that was—"

"You promised, Lizzie!" Jessica interrupted. "No lectures. Besides, who walks around with their diary, anyway? I thought it was just another notebook. I think Maria was relieved to share her secret with someone. I mean, she was mad at first, but she got over it quickly." Jessica gave Elizabeth an angelic smile. "Gotta run," she said before Elizabeth could ask any more questions.

As she watched Jessica dart away, all of Elizabeth's uneasiness about Maria's undercover work came back to her. She and Jessica must have read the same story in Maria's red notebook, but Jessica had thought it was real—she had thought it was Maria's diary. Had Jessica started those rumors about Maria's movie? And were they even true?

If they weren't, wouldn't Maria just have cleared up the mistake? Something definitely didn't make sense.

Elizabeth finished setting the table and ran to the living room, where Mrs. Wakefield was sitting at her desk, paying bills.

"How long till dinner, Mom?" she asked.

"Oh, maybe forty-five minutes, honey. Why?"

"I'm going to ride my bike over to Maria Slater's house," Elizabeth said, a determined gleam in her eye. "I've got some detective work to do."

Elizabeth parked her bike in the Slaters' driveway and knocked on their front door.

Nina opened the door. "Hi, Elizabeth! Did you come by for an encore performance of *Romeo and Juliet*?"

"Not really. I—I wanted to talk to Maria about some *Sixers* article ideas I had."

"Unfortunately, you just missed her," Nina said. "She and my mom ran over to the store to pick up some things for dinner. But why don't you come inside and wait? They should be home any minute."

Elizabeth followed Nina into the kitchen. "I hope you don't mind watching me set the table," Nina said. "It's my turn, and I promised my mom I'd have it done by the time she got back."

Elizabeth laughed. "I just finished setting the table at my own house. Why don't I give you a hand?"

"Thanks," Nina said, passing Elizabeth a handful of silverware. "I keep trying to con Maria into doing my share of the table setting, but she just won't go for it. When she was smaller, I used to get her to do all my chores."

"You sound just like Jessica!" Elizabeth said, laughing.

"I'll bet you two are very close, being twins and all," Nina said.

Elizabeth nodded. "We tell each other everything."

"Everything?" Nina asked, gazing intently at Elizabeth.

"Well, *almost* everything."

Nina sat down on one of the kitchen chairs, lost in thought. "Elizabeth?" she said softly. "Did Jessica tell you anything about . . ."

"About Maria?" Elizabeth finished. "Nina, there's something going on, isn't there? Some kind of misunderstanding?"

"A *big* misunderstanding." Nina nodded grimly. "A whopper."

"Did Jessica read something Maria had written and get the wrong impression?"

Nina chewed on her bottom lip nervously.

"I'm not sure I should be telling you all this, Elizabeth. But I have the feeling that I can trust you."

"You can. Maria is my friend."

"Good." Nina sighed. "Because pretty soon my little sister's going to need all the friends she can get."

Twelve

◇

Thursday morning, Maria had to force herself to enter the front doors of the school. There were only two more days until the yacht party, and she knew she had to come to a decision soon. Nina was right, of course. She had to tell everyone the truth. But when? And how?

Slowly Maria walked down the hall. Her feet dragged as if her shoes were made of lead. Behind her someone called her name.

Reluctantly she turned around. It was an older girl whom Maria had never met. "Is it true that you and Nick England are secretly engaged and are going to marry when you turn eighteen?" the girl asked.

Maria laughed in spite of herself. The rumors were running wild now. Nothing surprised her anymore. "Actually, we're secretly married," she snapped. "Not that it's any of your business."

The girl gasped and dashed off down the hall.

Maria shrugged. What did she care anymore? Her life was already ruined.

She headed down the hall and noticed a small group of students gathered around a large rectangular box. When she got closer, she realized what was inside. It was the new edition of the *Sixers*!

Maria ran to the box and grabbed one of the papers. There on the front page was her article, just as Elizabeth had promised. *Drama Club Seeks Undiscovered Talent*, the headline read, *by Maria Slater*.

"So how does it feel to see your name in print?"

Maria turned to see Elizabeth standing beside her, grinning. "Not bad," Maria replied. "Not bad at all." For the first time all morning, she smiled.

"You did a great job," Elizabeth said sincerely. "I'm looking forward to seeing many more Maria Slater stories. You are planning to keep working for the *Sixers*, aren't you?"

Maria's smile faded. "As long as I'm here," she answered quietly. "Assuming the movie doesn't take up too much of my time."

"Hey, I have an idea!" Elizabeth said suddenly. "Let's celebrate your first article with a Casey's Colossus!"

"A what?"

"It's a triple hot-fudge sundae. The biggest Casey's makes. Have you ever been there?"

Maria shook her head. How could she tell Elizabeth nicely that celebrating was the *last* thing she felt like doing that day?

"Then it's settled. We'll go right after school, OK?"

"Elizabeth, I don't think today's a very good day—" Maria began.

"I won't take no for an answer!" Elizabeth insisted cheerfully. Suddenly her eyes opened wide. "Don't tell me you don't like ice cream."

Maria managed her second smile of the day. "Actually, I've been known to eat an entire gallon of ice cream in one sitting!"

Elizabeth laughed. "See you in homeroom."

As Maria watched Elizabeth walk down the hall, she suddenly felt very alone. She really liked Elizabeth. Elizabeth was kind and trustworthy—the sort of friend that only came along once in a long while. The sort of friend Maria didn't really deserve.

"We'll have two Colossuses," Elizabeth told the waitress that afternoon at Casey's Place. "With extra whipped cream and nuts."

"I really don't have much of an appetite,"

Maria told Elizabeth as the waitress walked away. "This is really nice of you, though. I've been wanting to see Casey's ever since I moved here."

"Because of your research?" Elizabeth asked quietly.

"No, because of my sweet tooth!" Maria replied. She pointed to an envelope Elizabeth had placed on the table. "What are you mailing?" she asked.

"It's an essay called 'Becoming an Individual.' A magazine's having a contest and I decided to enter. It's a topic I've given a lot of thought to."

"What do you mean?" Maria asked.

Elizabeth smiled. "It's one of the drawbacks of being a twin, I guess. Everyone thinks of you as half of a pair, not as a separate person."

"I never thought of it that way."

"It was harder when we were younger," Elizabeth continued. "Jessica and I even dressed alike then. We shared everything, our clothes, our bedroom, even our friends. And for a long time it was fun." She sighed. "But when we got older, things got more complicated. People always thought of me as one of the Wakefield twins, not as Elizabeth. I wanted my own identity. Do you know what I mean?"

Maria nodded. "Yes," she said seriously. "I really do."

"I suppose you've had to go through the same thing," Elizabeth said.

"All the time. People see you play a character in a movie, and they think that's who you really are," Maria said thoughtfully. "Or they treat you like a star—whatever that's supposed to mean. I'm really just Maria Slater, but nobody will believe that. You've seen how the Unicorns act around me."

"It must be hard."

Maria shrugged. "It's not all bad," she admitted. "I mean, sometimes all the attention is fun. But most of the time it makes me feel lonely."

Elizabeth nodded sympathetically. "It was hard enough being a twin. I'm not sure I could have handled the pressures of being a child star."

Maria met Elizabeth's eyes and smiled gratefully. It was such a relief to talk to someone who understood that her life as an actress hadn't always been easy. "It's not as if my parents forced me to act," she said. "I've always been a big ham. I can remember performing songs at my third-birthday party!"

The waitress appeared at the table carrying two huge glass dishes overflowing with ice cream. "Here you go, ladies," she said. "Enjoy them!"

Maria continued. "I guess acting has always been in my blood. That's why, when my career started to slow down, I took it kind of hard."

"Slow down?" Elizabeth pressed gently.

Maria looked away. *Let people like you for who you really are*, Nina had said. This was Maria's chance. Didn't she owe Elizabeth the truth?

Maria licked her lips. "The truth is, Elizabeth . . ." she began haltingly.

"Go ahead, Maria," Elizabeth said gently. "You can tell me."

"The truth is . . ." Maria tried again, feeling the words stick in her throat. "I haven't really worked in a long time. Nobody wants to hire me because I'm not little and cute anymore." The words came tumbling out. "I can't get work anymore, not even in commercials." She dropped her spoon on the table and reached for a napkin to blot the tears spilling down her cheeks.

"It's OK, Maria," Elizabeth said softly. "Please don't cry."

"It's *not* OK!" Maria managed between sobs. "You don't understand, Elizabeth. There *is* no movie. I'm not an undercover actress. I'm just plain, boring me. It's all a big, horrible misunderstanding."

"You didn't have to lie, Maria. We would have liked you anyway."

"I just got carried away," Maria admitted. "And once I got started I couldn't stop." She wiped away another tear. "But now I know I've got to tell everyone the truth. When I do, they'll probably hate me as much as I hate myself."

"I don't hate you." Elizabeth assured Maria. "And neither will anyone else. They'll understand."

Maria stared at Elizabeth. "Somehow the Unicorns don't strike me as very understanding."

"Give them a chance," Elizabeth urged.

"Are you going to be at the yacht party Saturday?" Maria asked softly.

"Of course! I'm your number-one fan!"

Maria smiled. "Thanks for letting me get this off my chest, Elizabeth. I do feel better telling someone the truth. But you were easy to tell. I'm not sure I have the courage to face everyone else."

"Of course you do," Elizabeth said confidently. She nodded at Maria's slowly melting sundae. "Now eat that thing before it melts all over the table!"

Maria picked up her spoon. "You know what the amazing thing is? Suddenly I have an appetite again!"

After school on Friday, Elizabeth and Amy rushed to the school auditorium to get front row seats for the drama club tryouts. To their surprise, the auditorium was already half full.

"Look at all these people!" Amy exclaimed. "I bet they're all here to see Maria."

"That would explain all the Unicorns in the front row," Elizabeth said.

Just then the velvet curtains on stage parted and Mr. Drew appeared. "My, my," he exclaimed. "I'm delighted to see such a turnout for our drama club tryouts." He glanced down at the clipboard he was carrying. "Please remember that these are beginning actors for the most part, making their theatrical debuts. Be courteous and polite, and please save your applause until each reading is completed." He glanced into the wings. "Our first performer will be Donald Zwerdling, who has prepared a scene from *Cinderella*. Donald will be performing the role of Prince Charming, and I"—he raised his voice to a high-pitched squeak—"will be reading the part of Cinderella."

Several of the Unicorns burst into laughter. "I'm afraid I'll have to ask you to control yourselves," Mr. Drew warned.

Unfortunately, during the middle of Donald's scene, Jessica and Lila began giggling so loudly that they had to run from the auditorium, tears streaming down their faces. They returned a few minutes later, more composed.

For the next hour, the crowd sat through

twelve different tryouts, but it was clear that most of the audience was there to see the famous Maria Slater.

"Next," Mr. Drew announced, "a scene from *Romeo and Juliet.*"

Mandy stepped onstage, looking a bit fearful. She climbed on top of a large wooden box in the middle of the empty stage. "This is my balcony," she explained to the audience.

"Where's Romeo?" Jessica called out, but Mandy ignored her friend's heckling.

There was a long pause. Suddenly a strange boy appeared on stage. He was wearing a large hat with a feather in it and a dark, obviously fake, mustache.

"Who's that?" Amy whispered to Elizabeth.

Elizabeth shrugged. "I've never seen him before."

After a moment, the boy began to recite his lines in a low, smooth voice:

> *But soft! What light through yonder window breaks?*
> *It is the East, and Juliet is the sun!*

The audience grew hushed, listening carefully to the odd, beautiful words. Even the Unicorns seemed to be mesmerized.

"Mandy and this guy are great together!" Amy whispered.

Suddenly, halfway through the scene, Mandy jumped off her box with a loud thud. The audience gaped in surprise. Only Mr. Drew seemed unperturbed.

Mandy ran over to the boy, seized his hat, and dropped it onto her own head. Then she ripped his mustache right off his face.

"That's Maria!" Elizabeth cried in amazement. "Maria is Romeo!"

"Not anymore," Amy said, grinning.

The audience watched as Maria leapt onto the wooden box and Mandy knelt next to it. Mandy began to recite Romeo's lines and Maria transformed into Juliet, with a high, sweet voice and a shy smile.

When the scene was over, the audience stood up and applauded. Mandy and Maria took a long, low bow, and Maria waved at Elizabeth and Amy.

"They were incredible!" Amy said as she clapped.

"That's for sure!" Elizabeth agreed, laughing. She was happy for Maria's success, but she knew that her most challenging performance was yet to come.

Thirteen

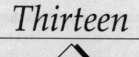

"So *this* is puce," Jessica murmured as Lila took her on the royal tour of her father's yacht Saturday evening.

"Isn't it divine?" Lila said, running her hands over the luxurious upholstery in the main cabin.

"Not bad," Jessica said. "Especially with the purple crepe paper."

"Who made the sign?" Ellen asked.

"I did," Jessica said proudly. "What do you think?"

" 'Welcome to Sweet Valley, America's Most Typical Town!' " Ellen read aloud. "I don't know, Jessica," she said doubtfully.

"I *told* her it was stupid, but she insisted on putting it up over the cake," Lila moaned.

"We *are* typical," Jessica said, jutting out her chin. "That's why all these famous stars are coming here to film."

"Has anyone seen Maria?" Elizabeth asked, joining the group. "I called her before we left to see if she wanted a ride, but the phone was busy."

"Just about everyone's here *except* Maria," Lila whined.

"And where's Kent Kellerman?" Janet demanded. "And all the other stars, for that matter?"

"They'll probably come in limousines," Lila said. "That's how my father always travels."

"I gave Maria directions so she could tell all the cast members," Jessica said anxiously. "I hope there isn't a problem."

"I just hate it when my parties don't start on time," Lila growled, glancing at her watch. "I'm going to mingle. You guys keep your eyes open for limos."

Elizabeth wandered onto the deck of the yacht. It was a beautiful moonlit night, and the entire ship was draped in tiny, twinkling white lights. It seemed as if the entire student body of Sweet Valley Middle School was milling around in their best clothes, watching anxiously for signs of Maria and the cast.

"Please show up, Maria," Elizabeth murmured. As hard as it was going to be for her friend to disappoint all these people tonight, Elizabeth knew it would be that much harder for Maria if she didn't make an appearance at all.

She was just about to return to the cabin when she heard a small voice calling her name.

"Maria? Is that you?" Elizabeth called.

There, making her way slowly down the dock, was Maria. Nina and Mr. and Mrs. Slater were close behind her.

Elizabeth ran to meet them. Maria was dressed in a beautiful black velvet dress with a white satin bow at the waist.

"I was afraid you weren't coming," Elizabeth admitted.

"I almost didn't," Maria whispered. "But then I remembered what we talked about at Casey's. I didn't want to let you down again. Or myself."

As Elizabeth led them to the boat, there were excited cries as people realized Maria had finally arrived.

"There you are!" Lila exclaimed, dashing over to the cabin door to greet Maria and her family. "It's about time!"

"Sorry," Maria said sheepishly. "I like to make dramatic entrances!"

"Where is everybody?" Jessica cried. "Have you talked to the cast tonight? Is Johnny coming?"

"Where's Nick England?" someone else demanded.

"We want the Buck!" another voice rang out.

Elizabeth glanced nervously at Maria, who was watching the swelling crowd like a cornered animal.

"I think—" Elizabeth called out as loudly as she could. "I think that Maria has something to say."

Maria looked at Elizabeth with terrified eyes. "I can't do it, Elizabeth," she moaned.

"Yes you can!" Elizabeth insisted. "You're an actor, aren't you?"

Maria nodded.

"Then *act brave!*"

For a moment, Maria closed her eyes. When she opened them, all traces of fear were gone.

Slowly she made her way to the center of the room. She held up her hand, and the room quieted almost instantly.

"First of all," she began, her voice wavering, "I want to thank you all for coming tonight. Special thanks go to Lila and the Unicorns for putting on such a wonderful party."

Lila waved at the crowd and took a small bow.

Maria paused for a moment, glancing at her family and then at Elizabeth. When she spoke again her voice was more confident. "I want to tell you a little bit about myself, if you don't mind. As most of you know, I've been an actress for a long time, almost as long as I can remember. I've played all kinds of roles in my career. I've met aliens. I've been chased by murderers. I've had cancer. I've even been a toilet paper roll."

Everyone laughed, and Maria waited until the room was quiet again.

"But there's a role I never got to play, and it's the one I've always wanted most: that of a typical kid living in a typical town, with typical friends." Maria gazed around the room. "The character's name is Maria Slater.

"When I first came to Sweet Valley, I knew how to be an actress, but I didn't know how to be a normal kid. So I kept playing a role I didn't even want anymore—the role of the famous star. I let you believe that I was something I'm not, and for that I'm really sorry." She took a deep breath. "The truth is, I haven't worked in a long time, and I don't know if I'll ever work in Hollywood again." She shrugged. "I *am* hoping to make the Sweet Valley Middle School Drama Club, though. Anyway, there is no movie, and there aren't going to be any stars here tonight. I'm truly sorry to disappoint all of you, but I'm not a movie star anymore. From now on, I'm just plain old Maria Slater." She smiled bravely. "*Ex*–movie star."

For a few tense seconds, no one spoke. The room was perfectly still. The only noise was the gentle lapping of the waves against the yacht.

Then suddenly, magically, someone began to clap. Soon two people were clapping, then three. All at once the whole group burst into thunderous applause.

Maria looked around the room gratefully, tears in her eyes. She ran over to Nina and gave her a hug.

"Well, what are we waiting for?" Jessica shouted. "Let's party!" Instantly the room came alive.

Lila was the first to approach Maria. "I have to admit I'm a little disappointed Kent Kellerman won't be here," she said. "But you gave me a good excuse to throw a party on my dad's yacht!"

"Me, too!" Jessica agreed. She leaned close to Maria and whispered, "Don't feel bad. You're amazing whether or not you're a movie star. Besides, I tend to exaggerate once in a while, too."

Elizabeth ran over to Maria and gave her a hug. "I knew you were brave enough," she said proudly. "That was the finest moment of your acting career!"

Maria couldn't help but laugh. "I kind of like playing myself," she admitted. "But I'm not sure it was my finest moment. Are you forgetting my amazing performance as both Romeo *and* Juliet?"

On Monday morning, Elizabeth found Maria and Mandy, along with a group of other students, waiting next to the door to Mr. Drew's classroom.

"What's going on?" she asked.

"Drama club tryouts," Maria explained. "Mr. Drew's supposed to post the list of actors any minute."

"I'm sure you and Mandy will be chosen," Elizabeth said.

"Cross your fingers!" Mandy said as Mr. Drew stepped out and taped a piece of paper to the door.

"You look, Elizabeth," Maria said. "I'm too nervous!"

Elizabeth joined the crowd scanning the list of names. She saw Mandy's name right away, but for a moment she couldn't locate Maria's. Then, to her relief, she found it.

"You're both in!" she announced. "Congratulations!"

Mandy and Maria hugged each other, then Elizabeth. "We did it, Romeo!" Maria cried.

"Congratulations, Juliet!" Mandy screamed back. "Hollywood, here we come!"

Maria rolled her eyes. "Oh no we don't," she said, laughing. "Sweet Valley is good enough for me!"

"Elizabeth?"

Elizabeth spun around to see Pamela McDonald standing close beside her. "I've got those notes I borrowed from you." Pamela said.

"Great," Elizabeth answered, as she watched Mandy and Maria dance down the hallway.

"Do you like my outfit?" Pamela asked.

"What?" Elizabeth glanced at Pamela. "Uh, sure."

"I thought you might."

Suddenly Elizabeth realized what she'd just seen. Pamela was wearing exactly the same outfit Elizabeth had worn on Friday! The same skirt, the same blue blouse, the same blue socks. She even had her hair the way Elizabeth had worn hers, right down to identical barrettes!

"But why did you *do* this?" Elizabeth stammered. Pamela gave her the creeps!

"I went to the mall Saturday," Pamela explained casually. "Actually, my blouse isn't quite the same. Yours was long-sleeved, and mine is short-sleeved. And of course my shoes aren't the same. I couldn't afford a new pair of shoes, too!"

Elizabeth shook her head in disbelief. "Why do you want to dress just like me?"

Pamela smiled shyly. "Because I admire you, Elizabeth," she said sincerely. "I want to *be* just like you."

Elizabeth didn't know what to say. It was fine to have someone look up to her, but this was getting a little ridiculous!

"Well, I'm really flattered, Pamela," she began, "but I hope you won't do this again."

"Why not?"

"Why not?" Elizabeth repeated. "Well, it's pretty expensive, isn't it?"

"I don't mind!" Pamela exclaimed. "You're worth it, Elizabeth!"

Elizabeth searched the hallway for Maria. Now it was *her* turn to get some advice. Maria would know what to do, Elizabeth hoped. There had to be a way to discourage a fan like Pamela!

Will Elizabeth let popularity go to her head? Find out in Sweet Valley Twins #51 ELIZABETH THE IMPOSSIBLE.

The most exciting story ever in Sweet Valley history—

COMING IN JULY 1991

FRANCINE
PASCAL'S

**SWEET
VALLEY
Saga**

THE **WAKEFIELDS**
OF **SWEET VALLEY**

THE SWEET VALLEY SAGA tells the incredible story of the lives and times of five generations of brave and beautiful young women who were Jessica and Elizabeth's ancestors. Their story is the story of America: from the danger of the pioneering days to the glamour of the roaring twenties, the sacrifice and romance of World War II to the rebelliousness of the Sixties, right up to the present-day Sweet Valley. A dazzling novel of unforgettable lives and love both lost and won, THE SWEET VALLEY SAGA is Francine Pascal's most memorable, exciting, and wonderful Sweet Valley book ever.

Be The First to Read It!

SWEET VALLEY TWINS™

Join Jessica and Elizabeth for
big adventure in exciting
SWEET VALLEY TWINS SUPER EDITIONS
and SWEET VALLEY TWINS CHILLERS.

☐ **#1: CLASS TRIP** 15588-1/$2.95
☐ **#2: HOLIDAY MISCHIEF** 15641-1/$2.95
☐ **#3: THE BIG CAMP SECRET** 15707-8/$2.95
☐ **SWEET VALLEY TWINS SUPER SUMMER
FUN BOOK by Laurie Pascal Wenk**
15816-3/$3.50/3.95

Elizabeth shares her favorite summer projects &
Jessica gives you pointers on parties. Plus:
fashion tips, space to record your favorite
summer activities, quizzes, puzzles, a summer
calendar, photo album, scrapbook, address book
& more!

CHILLERS

☐ **#1: THE CHRISTMAS GHOST** 15767-1/$3.50
☐ **#2: THE GHOST IN THE GRAVEYARD**
15801-5/$3.50
☐ **#3: THE CARNIVAL GHOST** 15859-7/$2.95

SWEET VALLEY TWINS™

☐	15681-0	TEAMWORK #27	$2.75
☐	15688-8	APRIL FOOL! #28	$2.75
☐	15695-0	JESSICA AND THE BRAT ATTACK #29	$2.75
☐	15715-9	PRINCESS ELIZABETH #30	$2.95
☐	15727-2	JESSICA'S BAD IDEA #31	$2.75
☐	15747-7	JESSICA ON STAGE #32	$2.99
☐	15753-1	ELIZABETH'S NEW HERO #33	$2.99
☐	15766-3	JESSICA, THE ROCK STAR #34	$2.99
☐	15772-8	AMY'S PEN PAL #35	$2.95
☐	15778-7	MARY IS MISSING #36	$2.99
☐	15779-5	THE WAR BETWEEN THE TWINS #37	$2.99
☐	15789-2	LOIS STRIKES BACK #38	$2.99
☐	15798-1	JESSICA AND THE MONEY MIX-UP #39	$2.95
☐	15806-6	DANNY MEANS TROUBLE #40	$2.99
☐	15810-4	THE TWINS GET CAUGHT #41	$2.95
☐	15824-4	JESSICA'S SECRET #42	$2.95
☐	15835-X	ELIZABETH'S FIRST KISS #43	$2.95
☐	15837-6	AMY MOVES IN #44	$2.95
☐	15843-0	LUCY TAKES THE REINS #45	$2.95
☐	15849-X	MADEMOISELLE JESSICA #46	$2.95

Bantam Books, Dept. SVT5, 414 East Golf Road, Des Plaines, IL 60016

Please send me the items I have checked above. I am enclosing $_____ (please add $2.50 to cover postage and handling). Send check or money order, no cash or C.O.D.s please.

Mr/Ms _____

Address _____

City/State _____ Zip _____

SVT5-7/91

Please allow four to six weeks for delivery.
Prices and availability subject to change without notice.